THE CAVEMAN IN THE BACKYARD

CHRISTINE KNOWLES

CONTENTS

ONE
CAVEMAN BY MOONLIGHT

KEVIN SAW the caveman standing in the moonlight. He knew it was a caveman because he had a bare chest, an animal skin wrapped around his waist, shaggy hair like Mrs. Bowersock's poodle when it badly needed a haircut, and he held a spear. At least it looked like a spear, but something was wrong. Kevin squinted and stared through his bedroom window. The spear was missing its tip.

The caveman was looking at him with the alert expression people get on their faces when they think they know you. Kevin did not see how it was possible a caveman — if it really was a caveman and not someone dressed up as a joke — should know him. He and his family had only recently moved to this small town in southern Arizona outside an army base where his father was posted.

The caveman shifted as if he was impatient. He

obviously wanted him to do something, but Kevin had no idea what. Then, to his surprise, the caveman walked toward him. Kevin had not been afraid before, but now he wished he could shout for help. His father was deployed and his mother was asleep, and if he called out his little sister would hear him, too, and might start yelling as she did when she had nightmares. And what would he say if he woke them up, that he had seen a caveman? It sounded silly, even to himself, and even as he was looking at the caveman right now. If Mitzi were there she would bark at the visitor, but their dog had run away a week after they moved here.

The caveman stopped in front of the window, the spear without a point held in his right hand. When he had first seen the caveman across the backyard, Kevin had thought he looked savage and cruel, but that had been his idea of how a caveman should appear, and this one looked a little wild but not at all hostile. He was brown as saddle leather, with a thick neck and shoulders. He looked older than himself, Kevin thought, but not by much, as if he were in high school, if cavemen went to high school.

On the other side of the window, the caveman was standing on the loose patch of soil where his mother had planted petunias. Once when Kevin pulled up his window and slipped outside just to see if he could do it, he had jumped down on the flowers and had to use his allowance to replace them. Kevin hoped the caveman was polite enough not to stand on his mother's petunias.

Kevin stared at the caveman and the caveman stared back. The backyard was bright as day. Moonshine glinted on the caveman's eyes like a flint sparking fire. Above them, his brows were thick and unruly, and now he pulled them together as if he was working out a puzzle. He reached forward with a finger, stubby with a little dirt under the nail, and seemed surprised when it bounced against the glass. Now Kevin was sure this really was a caveman, because everyone knows a window has glass in it.

The caveman opened his mouth as if to speak and then shut it again. Kevin desperately wanted to know why the caveman was there, although he doubted he could understand a caveman even if they tried to have a conversation. It occurred to him he might get paper and pencil and pass them through the window so the caveman could illustrate what he wanted to say. After all, prehistoric people were artists; he had seen some of their drawings on rocks, called petroglyphs, nearby and there were tons of paintings in caves in France.

Suddenly the caveman looked over his shoulder as if he heard something. Not wanting the caveman to leave before he knew why he had come, Kevin ran to his desk and flailed at the clutter on top of it until he uncovered a sketchpad. He found a pencil and turned back to the window. The caveman was gone! He pressed his nose against the pane, but he did not see the caveman anywhere. He tugged on the latch, finding it stuck like it was glued in place. He dragged his chair over to the window and climbed on it to get a better look. It *was* glued in place! He thought that it was an extreme measure on the part of his mother to make sure he did not go out of the window again and crush her flowers. He would not have been able to pass the pencil and paper to the caveman, after all. He thought briefly of sneaking out of the house to find him, but that might wake his mother, who could sleep through thunderstorms but not someone opening the back door. Kevin supposed this had something to do with being a mother because he could sleep through someone opening a door, but certainly not a thunderstorm.

He waited a few more minutes at the window wondering if the caveman would come back. He wondered what had roused him. It was almost as if the caveman had been waiting for him and had known he would go to the window to see him at that particular time of night. What time was it? He had not looked at the clock on his dresser when he got out of bed. Now he saw it was a quarter past midnight.

He shivered, even though he wasn't cold, and decided the best plan would be to wait until morning to tell his mother. He climbed back in bed, pulling the covers up under his chin. He thought he would lie awake all night after seeing the caveman, but soon he fell fast asleep.

TWO
FOOTPRINTS IN THE FLOWER BED

WHEN KEVIN WOKE he smelled bacon. The light coming into his room was so bright he thought he had slept through his alarm and was late for school. Then he recalled they were on a break, half of which had already passed. Suddenly he remembered the caveman, his brown face and unruly hair popping into his mind like dreams sometimes do after waking. The caveman must have been a fantasy, after all. He threw off the covers and stretched. As he put on his bedroom slippers — his mother said to always shake them upside down because a scorpion or a black widow might have climbed inside overnight — he saw his sketchpad on the floor in front of the window with the pencil beside it. They lay on the braided cotton rug next to his desk in the middle of juggling balls, a half-finished model of an airplane and the book he was supposed to be reading for school.

He ran to the window and looked out, but everything appeared normal. There was the wooden fence bordering the backyard where the grass was lush and green because his father had installed a drip system. A few feet beyond it was another fence made of barbed wire to keep cattle on the range and off the highway. A swing set and slide added an ordinary look for a family who lived in a house with children. Then he noticed a smudge the size of a fingerprint on the outside of the window. He began to quiver. If the caveman really had been there, he would have left footprints in the flowerbed! He ran out of his bedroom, determined to check it out.

As he passed through the kitchen on his way to the back door, he saw his mother and sister at the breakfast table.

"Where are you going in your pajamas and slippers?" his mother called.

"Outside!"

"No, you're not, son," she said sternly. "Not until you have breakfast and change."

"But Mom, listen! I saw a caveman on the other side of my window last night and I have to see if he left footprints!"

"Sit down and eat your breakfast. I have to get ready for work. Mrs. Bowersock is sick, and I've asked Melody Mason to look after you."

Kevin straightened up and puffed out his chest as he had seen his father do when he put on his uniform.

He said, "I'll take care of us today. After all, I'm in middle school!"

"I don't think a boy who claims to have seen a caveman in the backyard when he should have been asleep is old enough to stay by himself with his sister. It must have been a dream. You are always having crazy ones."

"But Mom, the caveman was real! I can prove it!"

"I saw a dinosaur," Savannah piped up

"No you didn't!" he shouted at her, losing his cool.

Savannah often said the same thing, or almost the same thing, as he did just to call attention to herself. This made Kevin angry, and because he couldn't punch his sister as he sometimes did the boys at school, he would storm off to his room and slam the door. When his father asked him to explain his bad conduct, Kevin said it was because Savannah wanted to make what *she* said sound more important. His father replied it was because his little sister looked up to him and wanted to do the same, or think the same, herself. Kevin figured this might be true, but it was still annoying.

"Children, please," sighed his mother, getting up. She placed a plate of bacon in front of Kevin. "Don't you think I have enough to think of without worrying about a caveman?"

"I did, too, see a dinosaur!" Savannah whispered.

Kevin sat down at his usual place, fuming. Now he

was mad at his mother not only because she dismissed his report of a midnight visitor, but also because she didn't insist Savannah's dinosaur was in her imagination, too. He had to express his frustration somehow, so he made loud chomping noises as he ate his bacon.

"Kevin!" his mother said. "Apologize for being rude or go to your room."

Kevin pushed his chair back with a satisfyingly loud squeak on the floor. When he reached his room he stomped around it for a while, but then he began to wish he had not behaved so badly because he really was hungry, and he could hear the clatter of breakfast dishes being washed and put away. He sat down on the bed and looked out of his window.

In the blue sky the sun was a giant, yellow disk glowing like a slow-heating burner on a stovetop, making the temperature rise throughout the day. His mother said it didn't rain very often where they lived now, which explained the stretches of wavy brown grasses and the gray-blue mountains dotted with scrubby shrubs surrounding them on three sides. Most houses had cement or stone walls around them to keep out wild animals such as javalina, which looked like ferocious pigs with tusks, and coyotes and sometimes a mountain lion, but his parents had wanted a view. From the back of the house they could see for miles, almost all the way to Interstate 10, and if you went west on that you would arrive in Tucson.

Now some clouds puffed up over the mountains and raced in front of the wind, looking like whitecaps, reminding him of the ocean at Turtle Beach, his favorite beach on Oahu. Before moving here, they had lived in Hawaii. It had been fun to watch the surfers and play in the sand. Sometimes the big sea turtles would swim all the way to the shoreline and he could get within a few feet of them, their big, gummy eyes rolling his way, not at all afraid of a human. Before that, they had lived at Fort Sill in Oklahoma, where he had been born. He did not remember much of Oklahoma, but he did remember Hawaii, which made him think of their dog Mitzi, who was gone; they had had brought her with them to Murray Springs from Schofield Barracks. He missed his friends, his school and the green mountains. Gone, too. Then he thought of his father, gone again. It was part of his dad's job, his parents told him, but it made Kevin terribly sad all the same.

His mother opened his door, dressed for her new job.

"Mom, don't go!" Kevin cried, feeling everything he loved disappeared.

"I have to go. I mean, I want to go to work."

His mother had a civilian job at the army base that had a name sounding like someone about to sneeze: "Wa-*choo*-ka." Kevin had learned it was written "Fort Huachuca," named after the nearby mountains. He was glad they lived in a town he could easily spell, Murray Springs.

"The people are nice and the extra money will make it possible for us to do fun things," she added.

Suddenly Disneyland—a vacation his parents had promised them when they were back on the mainland —did not seem like a good enough reason for his mother to leave.

"Melody will be here soon," she said. "No more talk about cavemen, please."

"There was just one caveman."

"Kevin," his mother said severely. "Your sister is six, and it is okay to have an imaginary friend at her age, although I think it's rather odd it's a dinosaur, but I expect more from you. When I come home this afternoon, I want Melody to give me a good report."

She bent down to kiss him and left. He heard her mutter something like "acting out" as she walked down the hall, but he wasn't sure.

He put on shorts and a T-shirt. When he came out of his room he heard Melody call, "Good-bye, Mrs. Sinclair," and shortly afterward the sound of his mother's car pulling away. He found Melody and Savannah in the living room. Like his bedroom, it had a window looking across the back of the house. In the distance, he saw cattle owned by Melody's family. Each cow had a brand called a flying spear on its flank, which was a spear with a design on its end that looked like wings. The

Masons lived on Spear Point Ranch, a mile or so down the road.

Melody Mason was only a couple of years older than he was. She did not treat him like a child but more like a friend, except when he got out of line with Savannah, and then she did not hesitate to scold him. She was very pretty with honey-colored eyes, each with a thin black border around the colored part. Sometimes when she was talking to him, he forgot what she was saying and just stared into them. She wore her long brown hair, thick as a mare's tail, in a braid. Every time she came to babysit, Savannah would pester her until she braided Savannah's blond hair, too; this had already been done when Kevin walked in to say hello.

"I'm going out to the backyard," he announced.

"Kevin saw a caveman last night," Savannah said.

"Really?" Melody replied in a tone of voice that indicated she did not believe it.

"I'll prove it to you! I'm going to see his footprints."

"Oh, Melody," Savannah interrupted in a pleading tone that always irritated Kevin. "Please paint my nails." She held up a bottle of their mother's bright red polish.

Savannah had a crush on Melody. On the days she babysat for them, he could barely get any attention. Still, it was much more fun to have Melody here than Mrs. Bowersock, who looked as old as his grandmother did and who by now would have had them doing lessons in workbooks she bought at Walmart.

"We'll be there in a minute," Melody said.

"Well, I'm going outside *now*."

He bolted down the hall and into the kitchen, where he burst through the back door, which banged after him, scattering some birds in a nearby mesquite tree. Under his window he bent over the petunias, noting with relief they were still intact. A fat black plastic pipe from the water system arched near them because his mother had asked his father to make sure her flowers got a drink every time the lawn did. At first he was disappointed because he could not see anything unusual where he was sure the caveman had been standing. He knelt down and gently parted the leaves. Right there on each side of one of the petunia plants he saw two very distinct footprints. He was so excited, he felt a little dizzy. He sat down and stared from one footprint to the other, and then he took off his right shoe and sock. Very carefully, so as not to disturb the ridges outlining the sunken footprint, he held his foot over the caveman's. To his surprise, it was not much longer than his, but definitely wider. The toes were short and had dug into the soft ground as if they were strong and flexible. Kevin supposed this must be a good thing for someone who ran around barefoot all the time.

He wished he had a camera or a cell phone, but his parents said he was too young for both, although most of his friends had them. Melody had a cell phone, and when he showed her the footprints he would ask her to take photos. His science teacher was always telling them to approach something new and unusual in a practical way. A picture would be proof the caveman had indeed been outside his window last night.

Melody and Savannah did not appear, and finally he could stand it no longer. He pulled on his sock and shoe and, without tying the laces, ran into the house shouting, "Melody, Melody, I saw his footprints!"

He found the girls in the bathroom trying to wash a spot of nail polish off the front of Savannah's white shirt, the one with lace on it that was part of an outfit their aunt, who lived out of state, had sent the week before. The clothes were intended for a special occasion, but Savannah had put on the shirt after their mother left in honor of Melody. Now it came out that Savannah had not asked their mother's permission to borrow the polish, either, so she would be in double trouble. She was crying.

"Melody, you have to come outside!" Kevin said. "And bring your phone!"

"Don't call Mom," Savannah wailed.

"I don't want Melody to call Mom! I want her to take a picture of the footprints."

"I can't leave your sister right now," Melody said. "You can help by finding some nail polish remover."

Kevin ran into his parent's bedroom and on to

their bathroom. The first thing he saw was his father's shaving cream on a shelf and his razor next to it. Even though his mind was in a whirlwind about the caveman, he paused and stared at the can. He picked up the can and held it to his nose, smelling a faint aroma of mint. He put the shaving cream down with a clatter and ran back into the bedroom.

"Dad!" he cried, expecting to see his father, but the room was empty and the bed was made as if his father had just left for Fort Huachuca, not the Middle East.

He walked slowly back to the bathroom. While he was standing there he heard a slight rumble and a faint sound of water rushing through pipes, but he thought nothing of this because he heard it every day at this time when he was not at school.

It was easy to find his mother's makeup with its lipsticks and compacts, and, sure enough, next to this jumble was a bottle of nail polish remover. He grabbed it and raced back to Melody and Savannah.

"Here it is! Now come and bring your phone!"

Ignoring him, Melody put a couple of drops of the polish remover on a cotton ball and patted it on the red mark. To everyone's horror, the tiny dot of red began to spread, finally stopping at the size of a dime. Savannah screwed up her face to cry again.

"I've got an idea," Melody said.

"What?" Savannah wailed.

"Later!" Kevin yelled.

"Let me see the rest of the outfit," Melody said calmly. "I'll find a piece of material to match and sew it over the stain. I think it will be cute! This is such a plain shirt, after all. We'll still have to tell your mother, but we'll tell her after it's done. Now let's go see what Kevin wants to show me."

But first Savannah had to put on her shoes, and of course she couldn't find one of them. By the time they went through the door to the backyard, more than five minutes had passed.

"No!" Kevin shouted.

Sprinkler heads had popped up every few feet in the lawn. As they watched, whirligigs of water shot out from each one, creating umbrellas of sparkling rainbows. His father had installed the irrigation system himself, and he was very proud of it. Not a blade of grass in the backyard was brown.

Kevin ran over to the flowerbed below his window. Sure enough, water had flooded the ground under the petunias. He should have recognized the sound of rushing water he had heard in his parents' bathroom. No trace of the caveman's footprints remained. He was so angry he felt his shoulders shaking. He grabbed the petunia plant where the caveman had been standing, jerked it out of the ground and flung it across the lawn.

"You're gonna be in trouble, Kevin," Savannah said.

Melody came to his side and stared down, clutching her phone.

"No one will believe me now," Kevin moaned. "I really did see a caveman last night."

"I believe you," Savannah said.

"You do?" he asked.

"If I can see a dinosaur, you can see a caveman."

"A dinosaur! I suppose it lives in here!" He knocked his fist against his head.

"No," Savannah said. "It lives over there."

Savannah pointed to an area east of them toward the Mason's homestead. Because the terrain was flat and mostly open range between Kevin's house and Spear Point Ranch, he could see a barn in the distance and a few dots that were cows or antelope, which liked to mingle with them. Not so far beyond the ranch was a line of trees bordering the San Pedro River, where his father had taken him once. He had expected a great flowing body of water, but it slogged along in a thin brown line. His father told him its glory days were long past, which he explained meant it wasn't what it had once been. Beyond the river was a mountain range where the famous Apache chieftain Cochise had sheltered with his tribe over a hundred years before. No dinosaurs lived there now.

The irrigation system shut off and the sprinklers popped into the ground as quickly as black-footed ferrets with a hawk overhead. The grass sparkled mockingly at Kevin. He started to walk to the back door when Melody stopped him.

"Do you really want to leave that plant on the lawn?" she asked in a voice reminding him of his mother.

Kevin had forgotten the petunia. He ran over and picked it up. It was still intact down to the roots. He dug a hole with his hands, and Melody held the petunia while he patted the wet soil around the base of it. When he had finished, it looked as if nothing had ever disturbed the flowerbed, least of all a caveman.

They went inside and sat around the kitchen table, unsure what to do next. Kevin remembered he had eaten nothing at breakfast except one strip of bacon.

"I'm hungry," he said, holding his head in his hands with his elbows on the table.

Savannah copied him, saying, "Me, too."

"It's a little early, but I suppose we could have lunch," Melody said, opening the refrigerator. Kevin and Savannah looked up expectantly, much as Mitzi had done when she heard the rattle of the dog chow bag. "But I don't see anything your mother's left for us."

Kevin recalled how tired his mother had seemed at breakfast and how easily she had lost her temper with him, although he had to admit he had given her a reason. Now he felt bad about it.

"She probably forgot. She's been worried about

her new job and Mrs. Bowersock," he said. *Dad, too,* he added silently.

Melody pulled her long braid over her shoulder and began to twist it, looking thoughtful. Savannah tried to do the same, but her braid was not long enough and it slipped through her fingers. Kevin wondered what he was going to do all day with two girls and nothing to eat. After the excitement of the caveman, his other projects, the model and learning to juggle, weren't appealing. As Melody began a search through the cupboards, he decided he might try drawing the caveman from memory and went to his room.

He picked up the sketchpad from the floor. It was a prize the principal had given him when his drawing won first place in his grade; the drawing now hung in the school library. His school was new and far out of town because more houses were planned for Murray Springs. His dad said this would ruin the charm of being away from the hustle and bustle of urban life and lower the water table, increase the need for support services such as police and fire departments, and make road improvements necessary, all of which would raise taxes.

Kevin thought adding a subdivision or two might be a good idea. Although he had made friends with two boys at school, Aiden and Jacob, they lived too far away to get together easily when school was out. Many of his classmates lived so far away it took a forty-five minute bus ride to get them to Murray Springs Middle School. Their parents were ranchers or worked on ranches, or were employed by one of the copper mines in the mountains, or were stationed at Fort Huachuca. No one could go anywhere here without planning and plenty of time.

He closed his eyes and the caveman's earnest face appeared. Again, he wondered what the caveman wanted him to do. His thoughts were interrupted by a knock on his door.

"My mom is coming to pick us up," Melody said. She was working on her learner's permit and had to be driven everywhere, too. "Mom's going to make us lunch, and you and Savannah will stay at our house until your mother is done with work. Grab some things you want to bring."

"Awesome!" Kevin said. Mrs. Mason was a good cook, and the ranch was fun to explore. It might turn out to be a great day, after all.

THREE

SPEAR POINT RANCH

Mrs. Mason arrived in a pickup truck, and because it was not far to the ranch, she let Kevin and Savannah sit in the back. It was a smooth ride until the truck turned off the paved county road onto the dirt road that ran a quarter of a mile to the ranch house. Kevin and Savannah had to hold on to the sides of the truck to keep in place on the hard metal bed. It was exhilarating to bounce along with nothing but the sky for a roof and to look backwards instead of forwards.

The Mason's two dogs ran to greet them as they pulled up to the house. The first time Kevin had seen them, he had thought they were wolves, but he learned they were Northern Inuit dogs bred from Siberian huskies, Alaskan malamutes and German shepherds. They were much bigger than Mitzi, and a coyote would think twice before it would try to have one of them for dinner, which is what their mother guessed had happened to Mitzi. The dogs were called Wyatt and Earp. Side by side, their names were the same as the marshal at the historic gunfight at the O.K. Corral in Tombstone, which was just up the road. His dad thought these were funny names for dogs and said it was particularly amusing to hear the Masons call out for Earp because it sounded like they were going to upchuck, his dad's way of saying vomit.

Kevin and Savannah climbed over the tailgate and followed Melody and Mrs. Mason into the ranch house, parts of which Melody had told him were over a hundred years old. The house looked to Kevin like a series of big and little boxes added over time to create one big rambling structure. He liked walking through it end to end, listening to the floorboards creak and stubbing his toes on the uneven stone slab floors and Mexican tiles. His favorite room was the living room, the oldest room in the house, where the first home-steaders – real pioneers! – had lived, all eight of them. It was hard to imagine eight people living in one room. He sat down in a chair next to the big fireplace and watched Mrs. Mason make lunch through the open door to the kitchen. Savannah and Melody had gone off to Melody's room.

A clock chimed twelve times, the front door opened, and Mr. Mason walked in. Kevin leaped to his feet, because his parents had impressed on him that he needed to show respect when an older person entered a room. Giving him a nod, Mr. Mason took off his cowboy hat and hung it on a peg near the door.

"Howdy," he said.

"Hi," Kevin replied.

He was suddenly tongue-tied. He had met Mr. Mason a couple of times, but Melody's father had not had a lot to say to him, almost as if he did not know what to say to children, although he had two; Melody's older brother was away at college. Mr. Mason was tall, made taller still by the heels on his boots. He was very slender, almost skinny, and his thick leather belt had the important job of holding his jeans up around his waist because they looked as if they would slide off if it were not there.

"Time for lunch, ma?" he asked, walking into the kitchen.

"Just about," Mrs. Mason said. She bent her head toward Mr. Mason, but Kevin could not hear what she said. He wished she would hurry up because the most wonderful smell of macaroni and cheese wafted toward him.

"Please call Melody and Savannah," Mrs. Mason said as she pulled away from Mr. Mason's ear. "Kevin, stop standing there like a jackrabbit in the headlights and come sit down at the table."

When the girls were seated and all of them served, Mrs. Mason asked them how their day was going. The story came out about the nail polish and the white shirt. Mrs. Mason looked severely at Savannah, who froze with her fork halfway to her mouth. Everyone else stopped eating, too, even Mr. Mason.

"Well," Mrs. Mason said after a pause to emphasize this was a very serious matter, "I am sure Savannah will never borrow anything again from her mother without asking her permission or wear fancy dress clothes unless she's told to put them on."

Savannah nodded vigorously.

No one mentioned the caveman, to Kevin's relief. He did not know much about ranchers, but he thought they must be very sensible people who would think he was out of his mind if they learned about his visitor in the night. There was talk about the mid-summer heat and how the monsoon rains were coming; a rodeo was happening in the next couple of weeks; and a purchase of new livestock from Nogales for the ranch was planned for the end of the month.

After lunch, Mr. Mason went off to take a nap because he started chores before the sun came up. Melody and Savannah disappeared down the hall without asking Kevin to join them.

"When Mr. Mason wakes up, I'm sure he'd like your company," Mrs. Mason said, and then she excused herself to fold laundry.

Kevin was left on his own in the living room. He had brought his backpack, but he had not had time to put anything in it, even his sketchpad, and all it contained were some old school papers. For a while he sat on one of a pair of sofas, and then he thought he should take a nap like Mr. Mason, although he was not a napping kind of person, but he had been up for a long time during the night. He closed his eyes, and in what seemed like no time later they snapped open. He looked around for something to do.

On one side of the fireplace he saw a bookshelf with a small table next to it. On this was a glass case, such as he had seen displaying things like rocks, dead butterflies or once a collection of small, brightly colored feathers attached to hooks, which he thought were the dumbest things he had ever seen until he learned they were called "flies" and were used to catch particular types of fish. He walked over to see what was in the Mason's glass case, and what he saw made his heart flutter.

At first glance, the row of five artifacts flaked out of gray, pink, black, white and orange stones looked like arrowheads, but they were not his idea of what Indian arrowheads should look like. These had sharp points on the tips and the sides looked sharp, too, but they were oval, not triangular. The longest and most impressive one was in the center, about the length of a forefinger on a grown man's hand and maybe one and a half finger-widths across. The bottoms of all of the artifacts were gently rounded in an upward arc, and he could tell they were intended to be attached to something. Each one had a series of numbers and letters under it in tiny block print. Kevin thought they must be valuable pieces because they were in the case under lock and key.

He jumped when a shadow fell over the glass.

"Those are projectile points," Mr. Mason said.

"Not arrowheads?"

"Well, an arrowhead would be attached to an arrow, wouldn't it? We don't know what these points were attached to, so we can't call them arrowheads. In fact, these points were made thousands of years before bows and arrows appeared in the Southwest. The shorter ones were likely attached to small handles and used as tools, and the longer ones might have been tied to darts that were attached to the head of a spear, or to a spear itself."

A spear! Kevin thought. So he was right in thinking the caveman had held a spear missing its –

"What did you call it, Mr. Mason?" Kevin asked, gesturing at the longest object in the glass box.

"A projectile point."

The caveman's spear was missing its projectile point! Kevin peered into the case, so fired up his ears were humming.

"Projectile points are found all over the world where we find prehistoric humans, but these are Clovis points. Clovis people were Stone Age hunters who camped near Murray Springs. The distinctive tools and projectile points made by the Clovis people were first discovered in New Mexico near the town of Clovis, so that's where the name comes from. These points are made of obsidian, chalcedony and quartz chrystal, all of which are found nearby."

The names of the stones sounded like a foreign language to Kevin, but it was a language he suddenly wanted to learn more about. He opened his mouth to ask another question, but Mrs. Mason walked into the living room. She flung up her hands and said, "Bill, you take Kevin outside to get some fresh air. I'm sure he'd like to see what's going on at the ranch, especially that new colt."

"I'll show Kevin the colt later. Right now we have some work to do on the tractor." Mr. Mason said this politely to Mrs. Mason, but Kevin could tell he was annoyed at her for interrupting him.

Kevin followed Mr. Mason through the kitchen and out the back door toward the barn and livestock pens. A small herd of goats, some cows, and a donkey called out loudly when they saw Mr. Mason. A flock of white chickens danced around Kevin's feet, so he had to be careful where he stepped.

Mr. Mason found a plastic bucket and a pair of work gloves and crouched beside the tractor. The big tractor was old and green and looked to be kept in good repair. Kevin asked if he could sit on it while the oil was being changed. Mr. Mason gave a nod of his cowboy hat and Kevin clambered up, arranging himself on the cracked black seat neatly patched with duct tape. He grasped the steering wheel with one hand and pretended to shift the gears with their big knobs with the other. When he grew tired of this, he remembered what he was going to ask Mr. Mason just before they came outside.

"What do the letters and numbers under the Clovis points mean?"

"They tell us where the points were found. When archeologists make an important discovery, they draw a map. The numbers under the projectile points correspond to coordinates on a map, so when an artifact is removed for safekeeping, we know exactly where it came from."

"Where did the projectile points in the glass case come from?"

"All but one of them came from a gully off the river a little over a mile from here. It's called the Murray Springs Clovis Site. They were found mixed up with extinct bison bones and horse teeth, some mammoth bones and tusks, and other stone tools used to kill and butcher animals."

"Mammoths?"

"Yes, they lived at the same time as the Clovis people."

"Would a Clovis person use a spear to kill a mammoth?"

"S'pose so. Say, you sound real interested in all this."

Savannah burst out of the back door.

"I want to sit on the tractor, too!" she called. Kevin was about to tell his sister to get lost because he and Mr. Mason were having an important discussion, but Mr. Mason swung Savannah up behind him. Frustrated, he slid off the other side and dropped to the ground, barely missing the oil can.

Melody had followed Savannah. Mr. Mason gave her a look and she said quickly, "Dad has work to do. I'll show you the colt. He doesn't have a name yet. Maybe we can think of one."

Dragging his feet, Kevin followed Melody toward a small corral inside of which stood a patient bay mare and a frisky black foal. Savannah caught up to them and ran ahead, scattering chickens like ping pong balls across the barnyard. The sudden activity made the foal whinny and kick; he streaked around the enclosure, his short tail waving like a flag. The colt's shiny coat reminded Kevin of something.

"What's that black stone called, the one in the center of the Clovis points in the glass case?" he asked Melody.

"Obsidian."

"Let's name the colt 'Obsidian'!"

You can't name a horse Ob-, Ob-," Savannah struggled to say.

"Ob-*sid*-ee-un," Kevin pronounced.

"Well, how about 'Sid,' then?" Melody said.

Kevin nodded, and so did Savannah.

Kevin helped Melody with her chores, which involved mucking out the horse stalls holding Mr. Mason's palomino gelding, Prince, and Melody's gray mare, Sombra. Savannah helped Mrs. Mason feed the chickens and pull weeds in her garden. Kevin thought the time had passed too quickly when barking dogs and a plume of dust signaled someone was driving up the road toward the house.

"Mom!" Savannah cried, barreling toward the back door. Kevin followed more slowly. As he passed by Mr. Mason, he noticed the rancher looking at him thoughtfully.

Inside the kitchen, Mrs. Mason was handing Kevin's mother a glass of iced tea. Savannah appeared from the direction of Melody's bedroom holding her white shirt. It now sported a little red cloth heart with a sequin at the center. Savannah began her confession and apologized for having worn the shirt and borrowed the polish without permission. Kevin could tell Melody had coached her, and Savannah was brilliant. It also reminded Kevin that this episode had delayed them from taking a photo of the caveman's footprints. He opened his mouth to say something, but his mother was concentrating on his sister and, besides, what good would it do to mention the caveman?

When Savannah finished, she lowered her head. Her performance satisfied the adults, including Mr. Mason, who had walked into the kitchen in time to witness it. Mrs. Mason handed him a glass of iced tea, too.

Kevin's mother said, "Mrs. Bowersock isn't well

enough to take the children tomorrow. In fact, it may be a while before she can. Melody, could you babysit again?"

"Of course, Mrs. Sinclair!"

Mr. Mason spoke up. "Why don't you bring the children here, Louise? I may even find some time to take them on a picnic."

As his mother nodded in agreement, Kevin grew very excited. He had an idea he knew where they would go.

FOUR
THE BLACK MAT

MR. MASON'S TRUCK, unlike Mrs. Mason's, had what was called an extended cab, similar to the backseat of a car; Kevin and Savannah sat in this as they traveled along the highway with open range on either side and the jagged mountains in front of them appearing dressed in a purple haze. An occasional cow flew into view and receded. Hawks floated in circular orbits before they dove toward prey, as unpredictable as shooting stars. Kevin felt the four of them were starting on a great adventure.

The caveman had not returned the night before. Kevin had stayed awake for a long time looking out of the window, but he had not seen anything at all, not even a rabbit. In the morning he'd gone outside to look at the flowerbed below his window, but there wasn't any evidence the caveman had been there while he was asleep. However, his fingerprint was still on the window, which gave Kevin confidence that he hadn't dreamed the caveman. He had really been there.

One strange thing happened—he discovered Mitzi's collar. On a walk around the perimeter of the backyard he found it lying on just the other side of the fence, and he wondered how he had not seen it the day before. It was bright pink, not easily missed, and he was sure it had not been there yesterday. He slipped it in his pocket and decided not to tell Savannah, because she would cry all over again about the lost dog. He would not mention it to his mother, either, because she had other things on her mind. They had not been able to video chat or audio call their dad since the night before the caveman's visit, and Kevin knew this usually meant he was on a special mission with his unit.

Their mother had dropped them off at the Mason ranch after breakfast with instructions to do what Mrs. Mason and Melody told them and not to trouble Mr. Mason with too many questions, looking at Kevin when she said this. Now Mr. Mason brought Kevin's focus to the present and the purpose of their trip as he said, "Where we're going is a National Historic Landmark and very famous because it tells the story of some of the early Native Americans that settled here, in Southeastern Arizona. We know now that humans had been on the continent several thousand years before that."

Mr. Mason turned off the highway onto a dirt road. The truck bounced and swayed. The picnic basket and cooler slid noisily in the bed of the truck, making further conversation impossible. A couple of minutes later, Mr. Mason pulled to a stop in a parking lot, which was really only a cleared patch of desert in the middle of nowhere, but there was also a fence with a sign and an opening to a path.

Kevin slipped out of the truck and onto the ground. Suddenly he was alert with a feeling that shot up through the rubber soles of his shoes. The Earth had been here for eons, which were further divided into eras, periods and epochs. From school and his internet searches, he knew an epoch could be broken down into millenniums. Each millennium was a thousand years, and if you strung twelve or thirteen of them together, you would come up with the number of years ago the Clovis people had been here. He had learned they traveled as far south as Central and South America, too.

"We're at the Murray Springs Clovis Site," Mr. Mason said. "It was discovered nearly sixty years ago by two anthropologists, C. Vance Haynes, Jr., and Peter Mehringer. Not too far from here, a rancher named Ed Lehner uncovered what turned out to be mammoth and ancient bison bones. It gave the professors a hunch there were more discoveries to be made in this area. We're going to see the clue that showed the men where to dig."

As they walked toward the entrance of the archeological site, Kevin thought of the caveman again and looked around. There were no caves that he could see, only great gullies in the ground the locals called arroyos or sometimes draws; roaring waters created them during the summer monsoon season. He wondered if the caveman had come from here. He thought it would be nice if he had a name—not Clovis man or prehistoric human, because these names sounded too scientific and all about dead people. His caveman was very much alive.

Mr. Mason sternly warned them not to touch any artifacts or fossils they might see because the Clovis site was protected by law. If they did notice something they thought might be important, they were to tell him and he would contact the authorities responsible for the site. With a caution to look out for snakes, Mr. Mason led them through the opening in the fence and along a path that wound through low cacti and bushes, some of them with thorns.

Savannah looked a little green from the bumpy truck ride. She was already acting Savannah-ish: complaining she was thirsty, there wasn't much to see, and how much farther did they have to go before they could have lunch? Melody handed her a water bottle and adjusted her hat. They all wore hats; Mrs. Mason had seen to that. As usual, Mr. Mason was wearing his cowboy hat. Kevin had noticed at lunch yesterday—the only time he had seen Mr. Mason not wearing his hat—that it left a band of pale skin across his forehead, and below that his face was tan as a cowhide. Kevin's baseball cap kept the sun out of his eyes.

Savannah hated hats, and she had only been persuaded to wear one because it was Melody's. As a result, it was too big for her and kept slipping over her eyes, and of course she walked into a prickly bush and stopped to cry. Exasperated, Kevin said to her, "Come on, Savannah! Don't be a baby!" When Mr. Mason and Melody did not give her any sympathy, either, she sniffled and shuffled along after them, considerably more careful.

They reached the lip of a gully. Mr. Mason walked down the steep slope, telling them a bridge had been here once but had fallen into disrepair over the years and had been hauled away. When he reached the bottom his head was a few inches below the ground where the three children stood above him. He helped each one down the incline, small stones and dirt bouncing loose from under their sinking footsteps. Then he led them deep into the arroyo and finally stopped in front of a wall of layers of colored earth with a distinct black line dividing it into two sections. The bottom half was maybe five feet high, and the top half looked about two and a half feet.

"This is the black mat," Mr. Mason said, pointing to the line.

The black mat was no more than a couple of

inches thick and ran for some distance on both sides of the arroyo, although at certain points it disappeared where the wall had eroded.

"Remember I told you that bones from Ice Age mammals were discovered just south of here on a ranch that was owned by Mr. Lehner? Dr. Haynes and Dr. Mehringer identified the black mat there first. When looking for clues that other ancient bison and mammoth kill sites might be nearby, the anthropologists discovered the black line in front of you now. The black mat indicates that many thousands of years ago this was a swampy area, called a cienega. The black mat is composed of plant matter and minerals that were common in southeastern Arizona during that brief geologic period. Clovis people lived in the moment of time just under the black mat when there were lakes, grasslands and tall trees here, capable of supporting megafauna—which is what large, prehistoric animals are called."

"What happened to the megafauna?" Kevin asked, suddenly worried as he thought about disappearing dogs, fathers, and memories of sea turtles, which were already fading. He reached in his pocket and touched Mitzi's collar.

"Temperatures got higher and the wetlands dried up," Mr. Mason explained. "Clovis people and megafauna disappeared about the same time. This took only a couple of hundred years when it happened."

"Sort of like global warming?" Melody asked.

"That's the theory scientists agree on most, although some blame comets or similar extraterrestrial events. Others claim the Clovis people overhunted and wiped out their own food sources. It could be any of these things, or a combination of all of them."

Kevin heard a sharp whine and suddenly a streak shot across his field of vision. At the beginning of its trajectory a light shone briefly, as if sunlight winked on reflecting stone.

"A spear!" he shouted.

Everyone's head swiveled toward him. Melody had been focused on her cell phone, shaking it in frustration as she tried to get a signal. Savannah could not see anything unless it was directly under the brim of her hat. Mr. Mason had been concentrating on what he had been saying, and after a pause at the interruption, at which he paid no mind, he continued.

"The two anthropologists decided to dig here and, sure enough, they discovered artifacts indicating evidence of a Clovis hunting camp. This site is special because it has given up more artifacts, Ice Age mammal bones and proof of hearth fires than any other Clovis site in the United States. Scientists can make educated deductions—that is, really good guesses—about how Clovis people lived."

There came another whine, and a blur of something long and thin arced through the air.

"There it is again!" Kevin cried, sure someone else must have seen the spear this time.

"I'd bet money that was a bird, Kevin," Mr. Mason said in a quiet voice someone might use to calm excitable people. Then he said, moving on, "Next, I'll show you where Clovis hunters killed a mammoth,"

Not thinking about what he was doing, Kevin turned around and ran in the direction from which the spear had been thrown, his shoes kicking up sand from the floor of the arroyo. In a couple of yards he rounded a turn, and the high cliff-like walls hid him from view of the others. A few paces on he noticed that the black mat, which had been on a level with the button on his cap, had begun to sink downwards, and he realized he was going uphill, making him puff a little to keep up his pace. A short time later, a cool, refreshing breeze sucked up the perspiration on his hot skin. Then moisture tickled his nose, noticeable only because he was living in the desert where everything looked and felt parched—and now it wasn't.

FIVE

THE CLOVIS CAMP

THE LINE of the black mat reached the top of the arroyo, but Kevin wasn't paying attention to it anymore, because just then he breached the arroyo's walls. He found himself running on flat land and had just a moment to take in the blue sky and knee-high, waving grasses before two huge beasts passed him, churning up clods of earth. For a few seconds, he could not see in front of him. Then he was aware of more animals and the sound of hooves pounding the earth. He sensed their huge bulks beside him and heard snorts and bellows. His instincts told him to keep running, that whatever herd-like creatures were surrounding him knew how to avoid him. Suddenly the animals were gone and he was staring at their brown haunches and their skinny, tufted tails streaming behind them. Bison, he thought to himself. He'd been running in a herd of bison! As the air cleared and he peered after them he saw on each head a massive horn spread, bigger than any he had ever seen on any bison or its kin before.

What a close call, he thought, bending over to catch his breath.

Suddenly he heard a sound that was becoming familiar. A heartbeat later a spear sailed over his head and plunged into the earth not two yards in front of him, where it quivered, giving it a menacing air. Kevin slowly turned around and saw the caveman coming toward him.

"Took you long enough to get the message," the caveman said, or something like that. Kevin did not understand a word the caveman spoke, but somehow he knew what he was communicating.

The caveman was shorter than Kevin recalled. He was wearing a different animal skin wrapped around his waist than he had at midnight in his backyard. This one had stripes on it as if from a tiger. From what he knew, saber-toothed cats had not lived in Arizona for a very long time. The caveman's chest was bare and Kevin marveled at the muscles on his arms and shoulders. His forehead was broad and sloped back to his hairline. A few hairs had sprouted on his upper lip and chin. He was not quite a man yet, but certainly not a boy, either. His skin was paler than Kevin remembered by moonlight, and appeared a glowing almond color in the bright, prehistoric sun, because he was beginning to suspect he had gone far back in time. He was surprised by how unsurprising this realization was.

"What is your name?" Kevin asked.

"I am To'meh Tilegon, To'meh of the clan Tilegon," the caveman said, pointing to his weapon and flexing his arm.

"Spear thrower," Kevin answered. "Can I call you Tom? Tom is a very good name where I come from."

The caveman grinned and pointed at Kevin.

"My name is Kevin. It's Irish. My people came in ships from a country across the Atlantic Ocean. They didn't walk here like yours did," he said, referring to the Beringia land bridge he had read about when he had taken his turn at the computer the night before.

"Ke'on of the clan Eyer-eesh."

"No, actually my name is Kevin with a 'v' sound in the middle and my last name, uh, clan name is..."

"Eyer-eesh," Tom said, turning away, and Kevin realized the introductions were concluded.

As Tom pulled the spear out of the ground, Kevin saw a projectile point of pinkish-gray stone strapped onto what looked like a giant arrow shaft, which in turn was strapped onto a long main shaft. He recognized the stone as chert, similar in color to one of the points in Mr. Mason's collection. This made him think of the large obsidian point in the same case with its groove-like black flutes flaked by an expert flintknapper and its sharp edges, both beautiful and sinister. As if picking up on this thought, Tom turned to respond, but emotion seemed to befuddle his answer. With a sigh he hung his head. After a moment passed, Tom indicated for Kevin to follow him.

As they went along, Kevin had a chance to look around. The ground was flat like that surrounding his house and the Mason ranch. To the west he recognized the Huachuca Mountains, where the fort would be built one day, and to the east the Mule Mountains, where Savannah had seen her dinosaurs. There the similarity ended. This plain was not thirsty and studded with cacti and prickly bushes. Here, verdant grasses waved joyously at the sun. He saw a lake in the distance reflecting the sky; he wondered if this might be an illusion because there certainly wasn't a lake near Murray Springs that he knew of. Perhaps this ancient body of water had suffered the calamity of a warming world, too, and dried up. He looked back from where he had come and could faintly make out where the arroyo sliced the earth. Beyond it he saw the familiar San Pedro River identified by its thick border of cottonwoods and willow trees. He couldn't wait to tell Melody and Savannah that it had not been a dream, that he really had found the caveman—or rather the caveman had found him. But he wanted to make sure he knew how to get back to do this.

After a few minutes, a number of large, dome-shaped structures came into view. They formed a circle around a wide, flat area with their openings facing the center. The houses were made of supple tree branches tied together and covered with local brush and grasses lashed onto the frame. Kevin saw hearths scattered around for communal cooking. To one side of the central courtyard were four sturdy tree limbs stuck into the ground on which a cover of wide, palm-like leaves had been woven and secured. It resembled a ramada such as Kevin had seen around patio pools, providing shade while allowing the breezes through, a welcome place to sit on a hot summer day.

Tom had brought him to what was obviously a camp. A crowd of men, women and children drifted their way wearing outfits of leather decorated with fur trimmings, feathers, tassels and beads. Most of the folk were barefoot, but some wore what looked like sandals woven from sturdy plant fibers. A few of the women did not cover their breasts. Kevin was suddenly terribly embarrassed, but no one else seemed to think this was out of the ordinary.

In return, Tom's tribe looked at him. Then an argument began. Tom bent to his ear and whispered they were debating whether he should be made welcome or not, being a foreigner. Although Kevin did not understand every word Tom said, he did get the message that he was accused of being different with his pale complexion and skinny white arms and legs, his black hair under his cap shaved close to his head like his Dad's, and wearing shorts, a yellow T-shirt and athletic shoes. Because he was different he was accused of being untrustworthy. Were there more like him, and if so, would they pose a danger to the clans? Kevin wondered how he was connected to these ancient humans. He could not recall his parents talking about any Clovis people in his family tree, although some of his classmates said they were related to Neanderthals because it had been reported recently in the news that a great number of modern humans carried this prehistoric gene.

A boy sprinted up to him with a huge smile on his face. The crowd stopped muttering and looked on with interest.

"Hello! You're the kid my brother was telling me about, the one who lives in a land far away, but not so far from here."

Kevin understood every word the boy said; he did not need to think as hard as he had with Tom. He wondered if this had something to do with them being close to the same age.

"I am Dher'sky." His new friend pronounced his name with a guttural middle syllable that Kevin knew he could not imitate.

"Then I will call you Davy," he replied.

Suddenly the tribespeople laughed. Looking around for the source of their amusement, he saw with utter disbelief Mitzi dashing toward him. As she reached him, she launched herself into the air and into his arms. Kevin hugged the small tan dog as she wriggled and panted, her long tail thwacking his stomach. He placed Mitzi on the ground and took her pink collar out of his pocket. She sat down obediently as he put it on, cocking her head to show she was proud to wear it, the rattle of the tag as familiar to her as the sound of her name. Then she began to growl, but not at Kevin.

Kevin stood up quickly as a stocky man with long black hair streaked with gray strode toward him. He carried a spear decorated with feathers and was dressed only in a loincloth and a necklace of sparkling stones and shells. He was frowning in a wizened face, and although it was obvious he was old, his muscles had the fullness of a much younger man as if they were in constant use and not allowed to grow flabby. He was much darker than Tom or Davy, and Kevin thought that might have to do with years spent under the sun running around half-naked. The elder man put his face close to Kevin's, the better to study him. Kevin noticed he was missing a few teeth, and his breath was unpleasant, as if he had been eating raw meat.

A youth about Tom's age followed behind the older man. His forehead jutted a little over his eyes, from which he gave Kevin a hostile look, and his lips curled back to reveal sharp white teeth, reminding Kevin of a wolf's grin before it attacked. The young man's features suggested he was related to the man beside him.

"This is Ke'on of the clan Eyer-eesh," Tom said, "who comes from –." But he here he stopped. Kevin knew in that moment that Tom had not told the old man, whom he assumed was the tribal leader, where he had been a couple of nights before. Kevin was not about to give away that he had first seen Tom in his own backyard, because there must be a reason he had not mentioned to the elder his adventure in the twenty-first century. Tom concluded, "Ke'on hails from where the sun is born each day."

The man nodded as if this made sense, and then he spoke for a while. Kevin did not understand a word of his speech, although he got the impression he was allowed to stay at the camp. The tribal leader concluded with gesticulations at the sky and toward the east.

The younger man added when the older one was finished, "But this one's hair is dark as night!" Then he averted his head and sent a stream of spittle to the ground. Kevin felt some of it hit his cheek but he did not flinch or wipe his face, although he thought this was the most disgusting thing that had ever happened to him.

Davy began to translate for Kevin what the old man had said, which was that travelers told tales of people with eyes the color of the sky and hair the color of the sun and called them the Fair Ones, although no one here had ever seen any. The Fair Ones were said to bring good fortune to the clans they lived with because they were descended from the First Peoples, which were gods or spirits, for how else could pale creatures with blue eyes and golden hair appear among dark-skinned people with brown eyes? Kevin wanted to enlighten Davy about all the different citizens of the world, but this did not seem the right time for a geography lesson, and of course all of this had a great deal to do with DNA, an explanation of which didn't seem appropriate now either. By the time Davy finished speaking he had confirmed that the old man was indeed their headman, Rescalispel, and the boy who was next to him was his son, Slatelispel, otherwise known as Slats.

Rescalispel walked away, leaving Slats face to face with Tom. The boys glared at each other and cocked their chins in a defiant attitude, all the while shifting from foot to foot like boxers about to send a fist into the other's cheek. Kevin could tell there was bad blood between them. When Slats finally followed his father and Tom stalked away in an effort to control his emotions, Davy explained to Kevin why Slats had spoken up about Kevin's hair: he was worried the tribe would think him the son of a god because his eyes were blue.

"My father's a soldier," Kevin said.

"What's that?"

"He's belongs to a—well, *tribe* of men and women who defend our home from people who want something we have, or who want to make us more like they are, or who just want to tell us what to do. When it gets really bad and no one can work it out, it becomes a war and then people get killed."

Davy thought for a moment; it was obvious he was not familiar with the concept of war. It had never occurred to Kevin that warfare had not always existed. As he looked around, he wondered what Davy's people would fight over—a few houses made of sticks and skins? They were a nomadic people moving on to the next hunting ground when this one was exhausted or to a better climate as the seasons changed.

"The elders quarrel," Davy said finally, "over the best routes to take and sometimes over wives, and even over who should lead the tribe, which is about to happen now." When he said this his dark face grew even darker and Kevin knew there was a story behind it.

"Our father is dead," Davy added. "Two butchering seasons ago at this camp."

Kevin did not know what to say. It was a great fear of his that his own father might die. They did not speak about this in their home, although it was on everyone's mind when he was away.

"Now you will discover the reason you are here," Davy said. "Let's find To'meh."

SIX

TO'MEH'S REQUEST

THE CROWD of Clovis people had dispersed and resumed their earlier activities. Kevin and Davy passed a few strong-armed men slashing at a large carcass as efficiently as any butcher Kevin had ever seen behind the counter in a grocery store. Other tribal members used stone tools to scrape fat and fur off the dark brown hide lying nearby. Davy said the creature was a bison that had just been killed. In fact, it was the last to be processed from a herd of eleven that had wandered around a nearby waterhole. He pointed to a stand of tall trees a short way in the distance to indicate where it was. Davy added that the waterhole acted as a lure for the animals they hunted and was a reason their campsite was close by.

A little way on they encountered a group hanging strands of bright red meat to dry on a tall wooden frame. They passed by women cooking over hearth fires, some weaving baskets or mats, older children helping their parents and smaller children chasing each other. Kevin had the impression this was a peaceful settlement, even though Davy had acknowledged that sometimes there were conflicts. He counted at least sixty people and then he gave up, seeing a few more on the perimeter of the camp and not including babies; possibly more of the community were inside the dwellings. Everyone appeared to know what to do and was industrious about doing it. The only odd note in the harmony had been Rescalispel and Slats.

On each side of the door of the headman's house two ivory tusks had been positioned, their sharp points crossing at the top. Davy said the tusks indicated Rescalispel's status in the clan and told him they belonged to a mammoth. Although he did not use the exact word, Kevin recognized the animal from his description. Astounded, he told Davy that mammoths were extinct.

"What does extinct mean?" he asked.

"It means where I come from we don't have mammoths."

The tusks were not so long and curved as those he had seen in drawings and photos. Davy explained they were from a juvenile mammoth because it would have been impossible to carry adult tusks from camp to camp. In fact, some grumbling always went on each time they moved because these were heavy and awkward enough as it was.

Occasionally as they walked along what looked like versions of jackrabbits and gophers popped in and out of holes. Lizards darted across their path, just as they did in his own backyard. Some things did not change much over time, Kevin thought, even 13,000 years later. Davy took them to a grassy knoll that provided a fine view of the valley. A herd of smallish horses with coats the color of sand galloped past. Their black manes stood up short and stiff, and their tails looked more like those Kevin had seen on donkeys than on horses. A little while after they sat down, Tom approached and handed out what appeared to be jerky. Kevin asked if it was from a mammoth, but Davy replied it was from a bison, which somehow made Kevin feel a little better about eating it.

He listened to the brothers as they conversed, but the only one he understood completely was Davy. It dawned on him that Davy was Tom's translator. As he chewed on his jerky, which was really quite tasty, he comprehended some of what Tom said, but any time Kevin detected emotion flashing through his brain it obliterated the message altogether. He heard the words "challenge," "lost," and "honor." Frustrated, he asked what was going on.

"Our tribe is preparing for the mammoth hunt where boys become men. This hunt is very important because it is a competition to decide who will succeed Rescalispel as headman," Davy said.

"Wouldn't that be Slats, his son?"

"It should be—!" Tom interjected, but the last word was lost to Kevin.

"The next headman should be To'meh," Davy explained in a tone that would soothe the most ferocious prehistoric megafauna in addition to a passionate brother. Kevin admired this quality in his new friend.

"We govern by consensus," Davy explained, "that is, with everyone in agreement. But if conflict arises, it is the elders who decide, and if that is impossible, we look to the headman. Our grandfather was headman before I was born, and Rescalispel is his younger brother. Slats is his son by his third wife, who is no longer living. When our grandfather died, his eldest son, our father, became headman.

"After our father perished," Davy continued, "To'meh should have taken his place, but he was too young. A council of elders elected Rescalispel our headman until To'meh achieved manhood, but now our great-uncle does not want to give up his position, and he wants Slats to succeed him. Elders from another clan, including our aunt, our father's sister, will be here soon to oversee the mammoth hunt to determine whether To'meh or Slats is more worthy to become headman."

"Another clan? There are more Clovis people roaming around?"

Davy looked at him with some irritation.

"You don't think we are the only clan, do you? We trade with many clans for shells and stones, ivory, bone and skins. We make marriages with their people and they with ours. There are as many clans as stars in the sky! Our mother comes from a place where the mountains wear white hats when it is cold. Inside the mountains, the fire spirits are strong. They push stones as big as a man's fist, or bigger, to the lips of the earth where they catch the wink of the sun and thus the eye of the flintknapper, who can pluck them as easily as berries on a vine and carve them into spear points, knives and butchering tools. To seal their marriage, our mother's clan gave our father a fine black stone that sparkled from within as well as without. He knapped a spear point from it that carries the life-force of the mountain inside it."

Davy paused, and Kevin realized what he was going to say next would be very important.

"We need you to find our father's spear point. In the struggle that cost him his life it was lost, although the shaft was recovered and is used by To'meh today."

Kevin recalled Tom in the moonlight in the backyard, the spear in his hand but without a point. A projectile point, Mr. Mason would have said.

"How do you expect me to find it?"

"To'meh is convinced you will be able to figure this out."

At that moment, Mitzi trotted toward them with a small green lizard in her mouth. It lay limp as if dead, but when she dropped it at their feet it sprang to life and scampered away.

"How did you find our dog?" Kevin asked.

"She came up out of the cleft in the earth the same as you. No one else knows it's there." Davy put his finger to his lips in the universal gesture for silence. Kevin nodded. He was used to swearing oaths and took the matter seriously. "When we saw Mitzi, we thought she was a dire wolf's cub just after it opens its eyes, but one of the women said she was already grown because she has nipples on her belly and her teeth are yellow—not sharp, white milk teeth. And, of course, there was the necklace," he said, meaning the pink collar.

Kevin said he was surprised the tribe did not include dogs. Davy explained some tribes did and some did not, but none of the dogs he had seen on their journeys looked like Mitzi. Kevin was worried about the mention of dire wolves. He had thought they existed only in books and on TV, but Davy spoke about them so matter-of-factly, he was convinced they existed here and now, or at least in the here and now where he was sitting.

"To'meh followed Mitzi out of our time into yours looking for the spear point. He thought he would find it in the riverbed where our father died." Kevin wondered if he might be referring to the San Pedro River, but of course Davy would not have called it that. "Our father died defending our mother from a –"

Here, Davy's description did not match any animal, living or otherwise, with which Kevin was familiar.

"It must have been carried off in the flesh of the beast."

"But Tom already has a spear with a point. I think it's made of chert," Kevin said proudly, displaying his new knowledge of the stones used for creating projectile points and tools.

"But it's not our father's spear point!"

Tom leaped up and walked away, scuffing the ground with his bare toes, his long hair hiding his expression. He clearly was discouraged that Kevin had not agreed immediately to the mission.

Kevin looked toward the camp. The Clovis people appeared to have concluded their morning duties. The sun was warm and had made them lazy; they sat in small clusters for meals or napped in the shade of houses and trees. He saw Slats looking at him from beneath the mammoth tusks. He thought about the visit by another clan's elders and the competition between Tom and Slats. He wanted Tom to win, but he had no idea how he was going to find a spear point missing for thirteen millennia.

Then it occurred to Kevin: Mr. Mason might know.

SEVEN

MR. MASON GIVES A CLUE

Tom and Davy led Kevin back to the fissure in the earth out of which he had come. He saw the grasses recently trampled by the herd of ancient bison. In the distance was the lake, the one that was not there anymore, and he heard the sound of the river rushing to the east. The brothers continually looked over their shoulders to see if they were being followed, but by the time they reached the lip of the arroyo they seemed satisfied they were alone.

The thought of asking Mr. Mason's advice had made Kevin cheerful. His attitude infected Tom and Davy, too, so it was with lighter hearts the three boys made plans to meet the next day. They decided Mitzi should remain at the camp because Kevin did not know how he could explain finding her. As much as he wanted to tell Mr. Mason, Melody and Savannah about his adventure, he knew he had to be clever to achieve his goal of finding the spear point. If they hadn't believed him about seeing a caveman, they certainly wouldn't believe him about visiting a camp of Clovis people.

He waved good-bye to Davy and Tom and charged down the steep embankment to the bottom of the gully until the line of the black mat ran along the top of his baseball cap again. He burst around the corner where he had turned to follow the origin of the flying spear, but no one was there. The tall walls of the arroyo jutted back and forth like a labyrinth. Suddenly he felt alone, small and lost. He wished he had brought Mitzi; at least she would have known how to get home. He wondered if the Masons and his sister had given up on him and left, but he decided Mr. Mason would not do that. Adults had the responsibility of looking after children. Then he saw Melody peer around a slab of the striated earth.

"There you are! Dad says if you have to take a pee, you're supposed to use one of the bathrooms in the parking lot."

"I didn't have to –" Kevin began and then shut up. He followed Melody, wondering how much time had passed, but it seemed only a minute or two had gone by in the modern world, even though he was sure he had spent a couple of hours in the prehistoric valley.

As they climbed out of the arroyo, he saw Mr. Mason and Savannah standing on a large flat area covered with scrawny plants and cacti. About forty feet away was a depression in the ground, which Mr. Mason explained had been a watering hole for Ice Age mammals. He gave Kevin a nod to indicate he was glad he had rejoined them.

"This is the bison kill site," he said. "We know Clovis people ambushed a small herd of young adult bison and calves here because of the archeological evidence of projectile points mingled with animal bones."

"How many did they kill?" Savannah asked.

"Eleven," Kevin said without thinking.

Mr. Mason studied Kevin.

"You must have been doing some homework about this Clovis site, after all, to know just how many bison died."

"No, sir. I guessed," Kevin said, wretchedly.

He knew himself to be a terrible liar. Mrs. Bowersock said he did not have a poker face. When he asked his father what this meant, he had explained that a gambler used this facial expression, which was essentially a blank one, so as not to give away the cards in his hand and provide other players with an advantage. Kevin respected Mr. Mason very much and did not want to lie to him, but high stakes were involved. How could he reveal to Mr. Mason that Davy had told him just a few minutes ago how many animals had died?

Mr. Mason adjusted his hat. The sun was almost overhead now and the day was growing warmer, just as it had in the Pleistocene. They heard a murmur of voices behind them.

"Visitors are coming. Do you want to see where Clovis people hunted a mammoth before we leave?"

"What's a mammoth?" Savannah asked, following Mr. Mason along the dirt path to a lookout point not far from the waterhole.

"It's like an elephant," Melody said. She pointed to the largest animal on an interpretive sign. Savannah stood on tiptoe to see it.

"When people think of mammoths," Mr. Mason said, "they are likely to think of woolly mammoths, but here in southern Arizona we had Columbian mammoths, which scientists think did not have hair on their faces and not so much hair on their bodies as their northern cousins. They were probably gray like an elephant, too, and their tusks were the longest of any ever measured in the elephant family."

"What happened to this mammoth?" Kevin asked.

"She was hunted by the Paleo-Indians. It's likely she was drinking at the pool when she was ambushed. The excavating crew at this site named her Big Eloise."

Mr. Mason scooped up Savannah, who was wilting in the heat, and carried her along the trail to a cleared space that served as a presentation area. A guide, whose nametag read "Jackson Griggs," was giving the newly arrived visitors a history of the

Clovis site. He held up an object that had a straight handle about a foot and a half long; at one end was a round shape with a hole in the middle like a doughnut.

"The original tool was carved from one mammoth bone," he said, "and used for straightening spear shafts."

Most of what Mr. Griggs said Mr. Mason had already told them, and no one objected when he moved on with a friendly nod to the guide, whom he appeared to know. Everybody knew everyone in this community, Kevin thought. They continued on the loop trail around the archeological site past a mound of dirt Mr. Mason called "spoil," which he told them was dirt removed from an excavation and not returned to it.

"And this is where they found evidence of the Clovis camp," he said, waving his arm to indicate a fairly large area. "The black mat is a couple of feet below us, and directly below that scientists discovered a hearth, tools and projectile points."

Kevin stopped, shocked. This flat expanse of small rocks and dirt, mesquite trees, and bushes with thorns was nothing like the flourishing green encampment he had just left. He looked in vain for the oaks and willows and the grassy knoll where he had sat with Tom and Davy. Chasms in the parched earth sliced by seasonal floods had carved up the landscape, leaving jagged scars. Cacti as shrunken and threatening as Rescalispel grew where the old man's house once stood.

"The workers found some mammoth tusks at this site, too," Mr. Mason said, confirming Kevin's observation. "They belonged to a sub-adult mammoth, which is a mammoth that has not quite matured, so they are not as big as some you see in museums."

The tusks should not have been there, Kevin thought with a sense of unease. The Clovis people were supposed to take the pair with them when they moved on.

"The sub-adult tusks aren't mentioned very often because the discovery of Big Eloise was much more interesting to the public. Where the tusks were discovered, right over there, some projectile points and shells were also found. The shells weren't from around here, although at one point mollusks lived in some boggy areas near the campsite. These shells were from the ocean, which of course is nowhere near here. That means the Clovis people were traders, too."

Mammoth tusks, spear points and Rescalispel's shells! Kevin was beginning to think the tribe was in for some catastrophe and he should warn them, but about what he did not know. He thought about turning around and running back through the arroyo that led to the prehistoric valley again, but one glance at Mr. Mason made him realize this would not be a good idea. Already he was walking toward the parking lot,

Savannah in his arms. Melody came up to Kevin and gave him a poke.

"Let's go. I've heard all of this before. It's so boring. And I can't get cell service."

They ate lunch on a picnic table in the pleasant yard of the San Pedro House, which Mr. Mason said used to be the ranch manager's house for a cattle company. Now it was a small museum with a gift shop promoting conservation of the area. Melody and Savannah went inside as soon as they finished their sandwiches. Kevin played with his crumbs and studied Mr. Mason's face, waiting for the right time to ask his important question. Finally he ventured, "How do you find a projectile point that's been lost for thousands of years?"

Mr. Mason looked at him as if this was the most reasonable question in the world and said, "You might want to start from where it went missing."

EIGHT

BACK TO THE CLOVIS CAMP

WHEN THEY GOT HOME, Kevin asked to use the computer, which was in the kitchen so his mother could monitor what websites he and his sister visited. As she made dinner, she glanced over and saw ancient bison, mammoths, camels and one she said she did not recognize.

"What's this called?" she asked, touching the screen and leaving a smudge on top of an enormous hairy animal with a big head and small ears, somewhat like a bear's, with massive paws with huge claws, and a muscular, long tail that helped to support it as it sat upright to strip leaves from a tree.

"It's a ground sloth," Kevin said, reading the print under the picture.

"Why are you so interested in these creatures?" she asked. Then she dropped a spoon dripping with beaten egg yolk. "Oh darn! There goes my clean floor!" she said and forgot about her question.

Kevin was relieved. His poker face rarely worked with his mother, and he did not want to confess he was looking up the creature Davy had mentioned was present when the boys' father died.

After dinner Savannah wanted to make a video call with their father, which they usually did several times a week when he was away, but their mother abruptly told her "no" and sent them both to bed early.

MRS. BOWERSOCK WAS RECOVERING, but on doctor's orders she would not be able to babysit anytime soon. Melody agreed to watch them until summer break was over. Kevin was thrilled because he wanted to go back to the Clovis camp. Mrs. Bowersock would never consider taking him to the Murray Springs archeological site. For one thing, she was quite plump and puffed when she walked and would not be able to manage sliding down the sandy arroyo wall to the bottom. Added to that, she would not have allowed him to explore on his own because she would not want him out of her sight. But he was sure Mr. Mason would take him if he asked politely. Savannah filled a shopping bag with coloring books and small plastic figures that seemed to migrate around the house of their own free will and were annoying to step on. Kevin threw some books into his backpack.

When they arrived at the ranch, Kevin noticed Mr. Mason's truck was not there. Melody told him her parents had gone to the fairgrounds in Sonoita, a small town about an hour's drive away. After that, they were going up to Tucson for some shopping. He wondered how he was going to get to the Clovis site.

"Why the long face, Kevin?" his mother asked as they said good-bye. "You were so excited to come to the ranch."

"I thought Mr. Mason would be here."

"Oh, Kevin," his mother said, "I know you miss your father."

He had not meant that he missed his dad, but now that his mother had said this, he felt it intensely.

"Your father's unit is on a special mission, which is why we couldn't talk with him last night."

Kevin had figured as much. They had an understanding not to speak of these things in front of Savannah, who could become hysterical. Their dad always made up some silly excuse the next time they spoke with him, such as the football game went on until late or the line for the shower was long. Kevin did not know what to say, so he hugged his mother. He felt her relax and knew he had done the right thing. He thought about Tom and Davy and how their father had gone away from camp one day and never returned. Something about protecting their mother, they'd said. His own father was away from home protecting his mother, too, only it wasn't around the next bend of the San Pedro River, it was halfway around the world. Across thirteen thousand years it was the same: if you loved someone, you wanted them to come back. He wanted to find out what had happened to the father of the two brothers, and he suspected the projectile point had something to do with it.

He waved to his mother until her car disappeared down the highway. Feeling dispirited, he went into the house and out the back door, Wyatt and Earp following him. He threw a ball to the dogs for a while, patted Sid the colt and afterwards picked his way carefully through the chickens toward the barn. Before he reached it, he saw something he had not noticed the day before. A faded blue tarp had been thrown over a big object. It looked as if it had been there a while because the tarp had dust on it and some of it was cracked in spots from the sun. Peering under the tarp he saw an old car. He would have stopped to look at it further if he hadn't been working up a sweat. Today was going to be warmer than yesterday, he had heard his mother say. As he entered the barn, the shadows inside were welcome. He sat down on a bale of hay and looked around for something to do. Then his eyes fell on a bicycle.

"Melody!" he called forgetting the heat as he ran to the house. "Can I borrow the bike in the barn?"

The girls were on the floor in Melody's room arranging dolls in a makeshift house under the dressing table.

"That's my brother's bike," she said. "I guess it's OK."

"Thanks! I'll be careful with it."

"Where are you going?"

"Oh, just around."

"Watch out for dinosaurs," Savannah warned. "I can see them through the window."

"What?" Kevin and Melody said at the same time.

The bedroom window faced east toward the Clovis site, the river and the mountains, but Kevin could not see anything unusual, certainly not a dinosaur.

"I did, too, see a caveman," Kevin shouted as if this was now in question.

"Prove it!" Melody replied.

"OK, I will!"

Kevin grabbed his backpack. As he passed through the kitchen, he saw some chocolate chip cookies cooling on a rack. He grabbed a few and, after wrapping them in a paper towel, stuffed them carefully in a small zippered pocket on the outside of the backpack. Any boy from any epoch would like a cookie.

He ran to the barn. The bicycle was in good condition, although he had to lower the seat, and the tires needed air. He found a bicycle pump and set to work. The tires on his bike at home were always soft from air escaping through tiny punctures from stones and cactus needles. Fortunately, these tires held pressure and he was soon pedaling down the driveway escorted by the dogs, which turned back when he reached the highway.

Soon he was riding down the bumpy unpaved road that led to the Clovis site. When he arrived he saw a few vehicles in the parking lot, including a white truck with an official design on its passenger doors. A man in a uniform like a park ranger's got out.

"Here for a tour?"

Kevin started to say no, but then he thought he might be questioned about why he was there unaccompanied by an adult. Mr. Griggs had not been in uniform; in fact, he had been wearing a T-shirt with Pleistocene mammals on it. Mr. Mason had said the guides were volunteers. A man in uniform meant business, and he likely had the authority to send him home or call someone to come and get him. That was the last thing Kevin wanted. Tongue-tied, he just nodded.

"Well, I'm not leading a tour. I just drive around these parts and make sure everything's OK. Mr. Griggs is already inside, so you'd better hurry before he gets too far along."

"Yes, sir!" Kevin said, throwing the bike to the side and bolting through the gate.

He ran down the path leading to the steep decline and slid to the arroyo's floor. The small tour group was disappearing to his left in the same direction Mr. Mason had gone the day before. He immediately turned right. With his heart pounding, he sprinted through the arroyo, around the sharp-angled protrusion that had hidden him from Melody yesterday and up the incline on the other side. The line of the black mat began to sink, the air became slightly cooler and fragrant with growing things, and then he was bursting onto the grassy plain again. He suddenly remembered the bison and looked around in a panic, but all he could see was a caravan of one-humped camels, each with a spiky mane and a short tail, moving in a slow, dignified line toward the lake. He knew from his research the evening before they were called camelops and were about eight feet tall at the shoulder. Then he recalled that dire wolves liked to prey on them, and this thought gave wings to his feet as he ran to meet Davy and Tom at the appointed place.

The boys were on the knoll with Mitzi, who wagged her tail so hard when she saw Kevin her entire body shook. They were very interested in the backpack, and Kevin showed them how to open it using the zippers. He handed each of the boys a cookie. They ate them in silence, the Clovis boys' eyes opening wide as their mouths adjusted to the sweetness. When they were done, they licked their fingers and Kevin did the same, although his mother would have disapproved and handed him a napkin.

Then he took out the books. He had grabbed one of Savannah's picture books, *What's in the Ocean?* He liked it because it reminded him of Hawaii. He showed the boys photos of fish, coral reefs, kelp forests, and sea turtles. He told them that on the island on which he had recently been living, the water was the same temperature as the air, and you hardly ever needed a sweater or a jacket, and then he had to explain what those were. The other book, *The Adventures of Tom Sawyer*, was his reading assignment for the break. It contained reproductions of the original illustrations, and the brothers were fascinated to see children about their own age and how they dressed a good hundred and fifty years before Kevin was born.

"And what is this?"

"A paintbrush."

"And what is that?"

"A picket fence."

And so they went on for a good half an hour.

"And what are these?" Tom pointed to the words when all of the drawings in the book had been gone through.

"It's the story," Kevin said.

"But I don't hear it," he said.

This reminded Kevin that he had stumbled into prehistory, meaning before recorded events. The source of news and storytelling for the Clovis people was oral communication. He began to read to the brothers from an early chapter of Mark Twain's novel. Sometimes he had to explain what a word or an expression meant, but even when he knew the boys did not fully comprehend, they were happy to listen. When he concluded, the brothers had dreamy expressions on their faces. Kevin had never thought of reading as magical, but now he acknowledged it was a very powerful thing. It was his own special skill, just as Tom's was throwing a spear, and Davy's was —well, Kevin was sure he would find out.

The book lay open to a picture of Tom Sawyer at a swimming hole.

"I think that would be a good idea," Kevin said. At midday, the valley was hot and a little steamy.

Tom had lost any further interest in books and become restless.

"This is all very well," Davy said on behalf of his brother, "but now we should think about why you are here. Do you know where to find our father's spear point?"

"Yes," Kevin said. "At least I know where to start."

NINE

THE HERO

IT IS a solemn experience to visit a place where someone has died, even thirteen millennia ago.

Kevin stood on the bank of the San Pedro River, which had been a good hike from the grassy knoll. This waterway was entirely different from the shallow, meandering river he had visited with his father in the twenty-first century shortly after they moved to Murray Springs. This one was robust and deep, and even the sound was magnificent with a tumble and slap that gave it a life as real as the Clovis boys and Ice Age creatures he had fallen among.

"Watch out for snakes!" Tom said, just as Mr. Mason had urged the day before.

Kevin quickly checked the lush vegetation under his feet, a little worried as he thought of the bison and camels he had seen, bigger creatures than those that roamed his own world. He wondered what size reptiles lived here. It crossed his mind that Savannah claimed she had seen dinosaurs again this morning. He was glad he was not that far back in time!

Tom led them on a trail along the riverbank under the shade of willows and cottonwoods. The path looked well-used by animals with split hooves and odd, three-toed feet.

"What we really have to look out for are…" Davy began, and he continued with the description of what might be a big pig with long legs and a long, curving snout. Kevin resolved to look it up when he got home.

"If you come across one and it's surprised, it may charge you, especially if it has a baby with it," Tom said. "That's why we carry these." He lifted his spear. Davy showed Kevin his knife with a bone handle and a translucent, white chalcedony blade. Kevin felt a little vulnerable with just a backpack.

Tom led them to a large rock that Davy scrambled up and perched on. One area appeared to have been chipped away with a tool. The rock had nodules of shiny black peeking out, bright as one of the spear points in Mr. Mason's display case.

"Obsidian!" Kevin cried, enchanted to have discovered the stone in its natural state.

Tom began speaking, but his words were in the ancient language and overlaid by emotion, so Davy explained.

"Our father discovered the black stone you call obsidian in this rock. It is unusual to find such large pieces in this valley. Mostly, there are small pieces the size of a man's thumb, only suitable for jewelry or disks for games, unlike where my mother comes from, the land of volcanoes and ice. Obsidian is valued for trading and my father, a craftsman known for his flint work, was very excited. He and my mother would come here every day while we were in camp and sometimes they would bring us, too, only on this day, they did not."

Using the bone handle of his knife like a hammer, Davy chipped a small fragment of obsidian out of the rock. He handed it to Kevin.

"Careful! It's sharp!"

Kevin studied the glass-like flake.

"Is the point you are looking for made from obsidian?" he asked.

Tom nodded.

Suddenly they heard a rustle in the trees. The brothers froze as if the most awful creature in the world were about to pounce. Poised to run, Kevin looked up and saw a ringtail cat, larger than he had seen in a zoo but clearly recognizable as one, and not at all ferocious. It was peering down at them with big, round eyes circled with white hair. It had monkey-like ears and a long tail with alternating bracelets of light and dark fur that it jerked back and forth. The boys had woken it from a nap.

The brothers laughed and punched each other as boys do when they've had a good scare and realize it was for nothing. A few minutes later, they were sober-faced and quiet. Kevin thought that even though they had brought him to where their father had lost his life, they were reluctant to talk about it. If he was to help them, he had to ask this awkward question.

"What happened here?"

Tom crawled up on the boulder and sat down next to Davy. He put his face in his hands. Davy leaned toward his brother until their shoulders touched, each clearly drawing strength from the other.

"It was the middle of the day," Davy began. "Mother was drowsy. Our sister was close to entering this world. As it happened, she arrived that very night! Mother lay near Father, who was collecting obsidian. Whenever you strike obsidian, pieces fly out like sparks from a hearth fire. Father asked Mother to move farther away for her safety, which she did and this time, truly, she fell asleep."

Davy continued in a low voice, saying their mother had slumbered until she heard their father cry out. When she opened her eyes, a large animal loomed over her. Davy described it the same way he had the day before. Kevin had not recognized it at the time, but now he knew it was a ground sloth. Kevin remembered the huge claws from the internet picture, but he had read that the ground sloth moved slowly and was a browser, which meant it stripped leaves from trees and shrubs. It was not a carnivore.

Above their mother, the sloth sat up like a begging

dog using its long, thick tail for balance while those huge, clawed forefeet hovered over her. The sloth was agitated because a saber-toothed cat was snarling behind it and their mother lay in the way of its escape. Their father picked up his spear and flung it at the cat, thinking it to be the more perilous of the two threats, but the sloth, faced with mortal danger, swung himself away from the cat's grasping paws, and the spear struck between its breastbones instead. With death cries and growls exploding around the rock, their mother rolled through the underbrush and hid behind some trees. Their father lunged to reach the sloth and retrieve the spear, but the sloth was lumbering awkwardly away on all fours. To follow him their father would have had to turn his back on the cat, a very bad idea.

It is rare for a cat to go after a sloth with its thick hide and fur pelt. The cat should have been at the watering hole near the camp, where it would have been a simple job to lie in wait for an unsuspecting bison or mammoth calf to come to take a drink. That day, the cat had traveled along the boisterous river seeking other prey, perhaps because the tribe had recently hunted game at the waterhole and their noise and activity had driven her elsewhere. She was frustrated by these humans who had come into her valley and thwarted her dinner. She turned toward the boys' mother.

Kevin was so absorbed in the story he did not

realize he had clenched his hands, and the one holding the obsidian flake began to bleed. He sucked his palm, ignoring the pain.

"Father's spear was gone, but he had his hunting knife," Davy said. "It was a fine knife, but not very practical to defend oneself from a cat that can leap and twist and has thick forelimbs like a wrestler's arms and fang-like teeth longer than a man's foot. He would have to get very close for the death thrust."

Davy put a hand to his face to wipe away tears. Tom looked straight ahead, stiff with the effort of not showing emotion, as older boys were inclined to do.

"Father called to the cat, which turned away from Mother. For a moment, the cat was distracted, snapping her tail with indecision. Then she lunged at Father, who stood on this very rock. They tumbled to the ground, Father on top of the savage beast, which had wrapped her front limbs around him, claws unsheathed. But Father still held his knife, and it looked as if he would win because he was able to thrust it upwards under the cat's ribcage. The cat released him then and crouched on all fours, her flesh hanging from her belly. Father struggled to his feet, his shoulders slashed with red stripes like the black ones on the cat. Taking this pause in the battle for life he looked at Mother and she at him, and the love in her eyes was as strong as a handclasp and made him bold again. He was determined that if he must leave this world, he would take the female cat with him and protect his wife."

The cat was severely injured, and she became enraged, giving her the immortal energy of two cats. She leaped again at their father and this time she was successful, slicing through his jugular with her sharp teeth and crushing his windpipe, but not before his blade found her heart. They collapsed together, rolling into the reeds at the river's edge where they were held in a death embrace as the water washed them clean for entry into the spirit world.

TEN

WHERE DID THE GROUND
SLOTH GO?

KEVIN HAD BEEN WITH THE BOYS' father, mother and saber-toothed cat during the recounting of Davy's story, and it was difficult to pull himself back to the present, or really, back to the Pleistocene banks of the San Pedro River. He could feel the presence of Tom and Davy's father as if he had only that moment disappeared under the water. Having heard his story, he would never forget it. He felt as if the boys' father was a part of him, too.

They left the trees behind with the river. The walk back to camp was long and hot over the grassy plain, and Kevin carried Mitzi most of the way. The boys walked along at a good pace. Kevin huffed a little to keep up, and he wondered where he would find the energy to peddle the bike back to the ranch. Of one thing he was certain, he needed to ask Mr. Mason where the obsidian projectile point had been found.

He had a hunch the spear point belonging to Tom and Davy's father was the centerpiece in the glass display case.

He followed the brothers through the camp to one of the thatched structures. Tom explained this was where women with infants and small children, widows and unmarried girls slept. Tom did not enter but called out, and soon a woman carrying a little girl emerged. Kevin knew immediately she was the boys' mother. She was beautiful in the way of the Clovis people. Her features were large, her eyes slightly tipped, her forehead broad but capped with thick dark hair that cascaded in waves around her shoulders.

The boys introduced her as Berul, which in their language meant Glitters like Fire in Ice. She gestured for them to sit down outside the house. The boys' little sister ran first to Tom, then to Davy, and finally to Kevin, who was still holding Mitzi. Using the dog as a medium of introduction, she patted first Mitzi, and then him. The family laughed good-naturedly. Their mother said the child's name and pointed to a patch of purple-colored wildflowers on the fringe of the camp, but Kevin could not grasp the syllables. A few of the women from inside, some holding babies, joined them. Coming from a society where people were physically separated by houses, jobs and school, Kevin was at first uneasy among the chatty group surrounding him. No one had issued an invitation; it was obvious they assumed they should be there welcoming the boy from somewhere else. Another marvel of the Clovis world, he thought, and relaxed.

Berul asked where they had been and when they told her, she frowned. The riverbank was as dangerous as it had been when their father was attacked two years before with the tribe hunting at the waterhole and vying for the same game with the usual predators. The band of Clovis people had fulfilled their need for bison meat; there was just the mammoth kill to go before they left for another hunting ground, but they were holding off on pursuing mammoth until the new hunter initiation.

"When will your aunt be here?" Kevin asked, remembering this would be the signal for the event to begin.

"When she arrives," Davy said.

Beyond the camp, a group of boys about Tom's age had gathered with a few adult men. Slats was among them. Each was holding a spear and something else Kevin could not quite make out. Tom said goodbye and trotted off, first giving Kevin a glance from under his bushy eyebrows to remind him to find their father's spear point, not to sit with women and children all day. Kevin made a motion to go, placing his hand on the ground to push himself up.

"Ow!" he cried.

"Let me see your hand," Davy's mother said, so kindly that Kevin understood every word.

Kevin held out his palm. The bloody slice was

covered with dirt. Berul took his hand and with her forefinger gently traced around the wound. She rose and went into the shelter and returned a few minutes later with a small bowl, inside of which was a green, slimy substance. She reached for his hand and spit on it to moisten the dirt and rub it away. Kevin thought this was not very sanitary, but no one else seemed to share his opinion. Indeed, the women seated around him looked on approvingly. Davy's mother scooped the salve from the bowl and onto his palm. It was surprisingly cool and gave off a faint menthol aroma familiar to him, soothing and antiseptic at the same time. Almost immediately the pain subsided.

Then Berul took a wide strip of leather, soft and pliable as a modern bandage, and wove it across his palm and around the back of his hand, taking care not to make it too tight. She continued in a figure-eight configuration until, to finish, she took a sharp thorn, such as Kevin had seen on some of the bushes on his rambles with the boys, and stuck it through the leather on top of his hand to hold it in place. She said something to Davy, who turned to Kevin and repeated, "This will keep your wound closed so evil spirits cannot enter inside you and do you harm."

"Thank you," Kevin said, wondering what evil spirits Davy's mother was referring to.

Davy accompanied him as they left the camp, turning a couple of times to look enviously at Tom and the boys on the opposite side throwing spears at gourds about the size of watermelons. Again, Kevin saw the odd hunting tool onto which the boys had now placed their spears. When a signal was given, the boys drew back their arms and then flung them forward, reminding Kevin of a baseball pitch. The spears soared and dropped like raptors after prey. The tool remained in their hands.

"What are they using to throw the spear?"

Davy told him. Kevin did not understand. However, he thought he had enough information to look it up when he got home.

"To'meh's the best spear thrower," Davy said.

Kevin could tell he was not bragging just because Tom was his brother.

"But he needs confidence. That's why he wants Father's spear point so badly."

"Like a lucky charm."

"What's that?"

"It's when you have something—like a ring or a stone or a rabbit's foot—and you believe it has magical powers, like a promise you will succeed in what you set out to do."

"Well, won't it?"

Kevin stopped to see if Davy was serious. He was.

"Of course it will," he replied.

Davy left him at the entrance to the arroyo. As he turned away, Kevin thought he saw in his friend's eyes a desire to follow him. He slung his backpack over his shoulder and began to run down the incline.

Finally the ground leveled out and the top of the gully rose above his head again. At this point he realized he had promised to bring something to Melody to prove he had been back in prehistoric times. He was pleased to remember he had stuffed the obsidian stone in his backpack. The leather bandage he wore was further evidence.

The arroyo was partially in shadow as if morning had passed into early afternoon. He began to grow a little worried about how long he had been gone. The day before it had only been a matter of a minute or two. Even though the Murray Springs Clovis Site had a parking lot and entrance gate, there was no lock on the gate and no fence around the perimeter. Anyone could walk up from the highway on a few paths through the rugged desert, and even loose range horses roamed here. As Kevin scrambled up the gully incline to the flat ground he saw a couple of them in front of him, swishing their long tails and gazing thoughtfully his way, not at all afraid. They were so unlike the small, prehistoric equines he had seen yesterday that he began to laugh. According to Mr. Mason, Pleistocene horses had died out along with mammoths, dire wolves, saber-toothed cats and ground sloths. These horses were descended from ones the Conquistadors had brought over from Spain. They were also a modern nuisance, leaving manure on the public paths.

He shimmied around the horses and ran to the

parking lot. It was empty. Someone had propped the bike against a wooden post. Guilt washed over him because it was not his bike, but Melody's brother's bike, and he needed to return it in good shape. Fortunately, he did not see any scratches on it from where he had thrown it down in his excitement to get to the Clovis camp. He jumped on the bike and began his return trip, careful not to grip the handle too hard with his injured hand.

By the time he reached the ranch he was worn out. He took the bicycle to the barn and wiped it off with a rag and then went into the house. Melody was making grilled cheese sandwiches. The aroma tickled his stomach and made him realize how hungry he was.

"That was a long bike ride," she said.

"What do you mean?"

"Well, you've been gone a couple of hours."

"I rode out to the Clovis site," Kevin said, thinking there was no reason not to be honest about it. "I looked around a bit more."

"Did you see a caveman?" Melody asked with a superior attitude, which of course implied he had not.

"Yes, actually I saw quite a few of them. Only they aren't really cavemen, at least not how we think of cavemen. Sometimes they live in caves, if that is where the best hunting is at the time."

"And you brought me something to prove this?"

Melody had her nose in the air—it wasn't just an expression, Kevin thought. He was getting annoyed, and his hand hurt because the exertion from riding the bicycle had made his blood pound against the wound. He unzipped his backpack and reached carefully inside. The sharp obsidian had made a tiny hole in the canvas. He held the volcanic glass out to her.

"It's just a rock," she said. "You could have picked it up anywhere, although it looks as if someone has chipped away at one side. What happened to your hand?"

"You don't believe I saw a caveman, so I won't tell you."

Savannah walked into the kitchen just then, holding a couple of dolls. She set them on the table and ran over to Kevin.

"I believe you! Tell me what happened!"

Kevin began with the story of the day before when he had disappeared during Mr. Mason's tour and what had occurred when he stepped into the Pleistocene. The grilled cheese sandwiches began to burn. Melody turned to the stove to flip them, but when her attention was once again on Kevin she said, "You're not telling the truth, Kevin Sinclair! That's wrong, you know. And you're encouraging Savannah to believe in dinosaurs."

"I did too see dinosaurs!"

"Come with me tomorrow," Kevin said earnestly. "They're friendly people. And you don't think I could have figured out how to bandage my own hand, do you?"

Melody placed the sandwiches in front of them. Kevin was so hungry he ate his in a few bites. He eyed Savannah's plate to see if he could steal half of hers. She ate like a bird, Mrs. Bowersock said, pecking away at it in bits and pieces.

"OK," Melody said. Then whispering in Kevin's ear she added, "Anything to get out of playing dolls again. But I'll have to tell my parents where we're going."

"Back to the Ice Age?" Kevin asked, incredulous.

"Of course not! They'd lock me up in the loony bin. But Dad thinks it's wonderful you're so interested in all this prehistoric stuff because he was, too, as a boy. My brother was only interested in things with motors."

"What's a loony bin?" Savannah asked.

"It's like a jail for crazy people," Kevin said.

"Are you going to jail?"

"No, stupid. I'm going to take us to the Clovis camp. But you can't tell Mom," he added as an afterthought.

Savannah's face reflected her struggle with being aware that not telling their mother where they were going was wrong. On the other hand, if she did not agree, no one would want to play with her.

Melody recognized the little girl's dilemma.

"What we're going to do tomorrow is just like playing dolls," she said. "You know, we really don't fly on talking unicorns with wings or go to fancy parties at the castle."

Savannah gave Melody a look of surprise. Of course they did!

"We'll go with Kevin to see the caveman and the Clovis people, and we'll have fun pretending we are back in prehistoric times."

Melody looked at Kevin with an arched eyebrow, indicating that although she had agreed to go, she still did not believe him, bandage or not.

"Pinky swear you won't tell Mom," he said to Savannah. She solemnly entwined her little finger with his, eyeing the thorn and nodding her head in agreement.

Suddenly Kevin realized his hand no longer hurt. He studied the leather wrap and wondered what kind of animal it had come from. An ancient bison? Was it from the hide of one of the antelope-like creatures hanging from a tree at the camp, looking remarkably like one of the pronghorns he had seen over the back fence of his yard intermingling with the Mason's cattle? Antelope was one of the species, along with ancient bison, that had survived the great extinction and whose descendants were still alive in the present day. As he studied the leather, he noticed it had begun to stiffen.

After lunch, the girls went back to Melody's bedroom, and Kevin hurried over to the display of projectile points in the living room. He held the stone flake Davy had given him over the black obsidian point. He thought they looked very similar and even reflected light in the same manner. Below Mr. Mason's obsidian point were the coordinates where it had been found. He had to ask Mr. Mason to tell him where this was. But to his disappointment, their mother picked them up before the Masons returned from Tucson.

"I've taken the day off tomorrow," Mrs. Sinclair said cheerfully as they got in the car. "How about lunch and a movie?"

Kevin and Savannah looked at each other.

"That will be nice, Mom," Savannah replied.

Kevin was so frustrated he couldn't speak. He clenched his fists and felt the bandage press into the injured flesh of his palm. Perhaps an evil spirit had found a way to get inside him after all and was thwarting his plans for tomorrow.

ELEVEN

MR. MASON LEADS THE WAY

KEVIN WOKE the next morning feeling miserable. He had asked his mother the night before if he could remain home while she and Savannah went into the city for the day, but she said—as she had said a million times before—he was too young to stay by himself without supervision.

"Don't scowl," she added.

"Your face will freeze," Savannah chimed in. It was a family saying that meant when you made an unattractive face, it would stay that way forever.

Kevin huffed with frustration.

His mother sighed.

"All right. We'll ask your father when he calls tonight if it's possible for you to stay alone for a few hours to begin with."

But their father did not call that evening, which

made everyone unhappy, including Savannah, who had left her dolls at Melody's house. When she realized this, she stomped around yelling that she missed Daddy and Mitzi and her only friends were dinosaurs. Then she began to cry. In the end, their mother allowed her to sleep with her, which their father disapproved of, but which happened frequently when he was gone.

Coming into his room to kiss him good night his mother noticed Kevin was favoring his hand and asked why. He had kept it hidden from her all evening, which had not been hard to do because she had been distracted by Savannah. Now he held his palm out to her, the laceration nearly healed. The bandage had dried up on the car ride home from the ranch, and all that was left of it was dust on the seat; the thorn had completely disappeared. Mrs. Sinclair held his palm up to her nose.

"It smells like creosote," she said. "Why would you put creosote on your cut?"

"I learned it in Boy Scouts."

"I didn't know Mrs. Anderson was so versed in Scout lore to suggest you put creosote on a wound."

Mrs. Anderson, their troop leader, was better at making lemon bars than teaching skills and building character. For example, she could never get a worm on a fishhook without pricking her finger, and then she swore at it.

"I read how to do it in a manual," Kevin said, feeling low.

The next morning his mother relented and allowed him to stay home. Before she left, she gave him a list of chores and instructions on what to do if something happened, such as if a stranger knocked on the door, he was not to answer it. Above all, he was not allowed to leave the house without her permission. Kevin knew this already but sat patiently as she lectured him.

While his mother and Savannah were getting dressed, he turned on the computer to look up the strange animal Davy had described the day before, the one that was supposed to be so dangerous, especially when accompanied by its young. He discovered it was a tapir. Adults could weigh up to two hundred pounds and were preyed upon by large cats, such as the saber-tooth, and also by primitive types of jaguars and lions. Lions! This was the first he had read about lions in southern Arizona. There certainly were a lot of dangerous animals to look out for back then. No wonder the brothers had been spooked yesterday at the river when the tree rustled. Good thing it had only been a ringtail cat.

Next, he typed in the keywords "spear thrower" and came up with an image of the strange-looking tool the Paleo-Indian boys had used. It was called an atlatl, but this name was not given to the device until much later, coming from a word in the Aztec language in Mexico and Central America. By whatever name, the ancient spear-throwing tool had been used in the Old World, meaning Europe and Africa, over 30,000 years ago. It had likely come to the New World along with the Clovis people.

Impatient, Kevin waited for his mother and sister to leave. Savannah dawdled as usual, but finally they drove away, their mother reminding Kevin to lock the door after them. He counted to a hundred to make sure they really were gone and did not come back for something they had forgotten, and then he ran into the garage. His own bike was sprawled over the lawn mower where he had pitched it a few days before. It had a soft back tire and he yelled out some curse words he had heard his Dad and his buddies use after a few beers when they thought he couldn't hear them.

He looked around for the tire pump. The last time he had fixed a flat, he had left the pump in the middle of the garage and his mother had tripped over it. She had stuffed it in the broom closet, threatening the next time that happened she would throw it away, but he knew she wouldn't do that. His mother did not stay mad at him very long, especially when his father was gone. He found the pump where she had placed it. Unfortunately, the inner tube was also punctured, and he did not have any spares. He was angry with himself. Wasn't the Boy Scout motto *Be prepared*? He walked around kicking things, but not hard enough to result in real damage and punishment. He had to get to the Mason's ranch somehow, and the only solution was to walk. He opened the door of his father's Jeep and took out the garage door opener; the other was in his mother's car. He raised the door and scooted outside, and then lowered the door and hid the opener under a bush. He'd use it to let himself back in when he got home, then return it to the Jeep.

Already the late-summer day was hot, although it was only a little before ten o'clock. After walking about five minutes, he regretted not bringing water. He stopped to take off his cap and mop the sweat from his face with the sleeve of his shirt. He heard a car approaching from behind. When he turned around, he saw the official white truck he had seen at the Murray Springs Clovis Site the day before pull over.

"Young man," the driver called out, "where are you headed?"

"Spear Point Ranch, sir," Kevin said.

"Well, hop in. It's hot and dusty along this highway. Not like Hawaii."

As Kevin had figured, everyone knew everybody here.

"Where's your bike today? I thought you might have wrecked it the way you pitched it down and tore off. I stood it up for you."

"Thank you, sir. I appreciate it. I, uh, left it at the ranch."

At that moment to Kevin's horror he saw his

mother's car coming toward them. He threw his hat on the floor of the truck and kept his head down until it passed so she wouldn't see him.

"You OK son?"

"Yes, sir. I thought I felt a bug crawling on my head."

When he reached the ranch, Wyatt and Earp bounded out to greet him, woofing wildly. Mrs. Mason's truck was gone, but to his relief, Mr. Mason's was parked in front. Mr. Mason walked around from the back of the house.

"I knew it was someone friendly," he said, "by the way they were barking. You can always tell with dogs, you know. You've been here so often lately, they think you're family."

Kevin was a little embarrassed. He wondered if he was being a pest, as Mrs. Bowersock would say.

"Your mother stopped by a few minutes ago. Savannah had forgotten something."

Kevin swallowed hard. If his bicycle had not needed its tire fixed, delaying him from leaving the house, and the officer had not picked him up, he would have been walking toward the ranch as his mother was driving the opposite way in the direction of Sierra Vista. That would be reason enough to ground him until he turned twenty!

"Melody and Mrs. Mason took advantage of the free day and went shopping. Girl time, they call it. Can I help you with something?"

Kevin had to get down to business. Tom's status in the clan was at stake, and he had vowed to help him. He screwed up his courage and blurted, "Mr. Mason, would you tell me where you found the projectile points?"

In answer, the tall, quiet man led Kevin into the house and across the living room. He walked to the bookcase, where he reached for an empty vase and turned it upside down. A small key fell out. He went over to the glass-topped case, unlocked it, and pulled out a drawer underneath the display, from which he took out a map. Kevin recognized the outlines of the Murray Springs Clovis Site. On it were four circles identified with letters and numbers.

"Here you see the areas where clusters of projectile points were found," Mr. Mason said, "And these symbols indicate what materials the points were made of: chert, chalcedony, quartz crystal and basalt." He touched the top of the glass to identify each point and then laid a finger on the map, indicating where each one had been discovered.

Kevin held his breath. There were only four circles on the map.

"And this," Mr. Mason said, his finger hovering over the black, volcanic glass point, "was not found there, but at a site farther away."

Kevin let his breath out so fast the glass top of the case clouded over for a second.

"Where?" he squeaked.

"It was a couple of miles south of here exposed in a gully eroded by spring floods, not far from the San Pedro River. I found it," he said, rather proudly for Mr. Mason. "I found it while I was hunting wild turkey when I was a boy. It was an important find for several reasons. First, the point was intact, not broken or chipped. Second, it was made of a black obsidian not known to these parts, but later identified as coming from about 250 miles north of here in a canyon in the Mogollon Rim. Although you can find obsidian in this part of the state, it's rare to find nodules big enough to yield such a large point as you see in the case. And the last thing that made it special was that it was surrounded by the ribcage of what I later found out was a ground sloth."

Kevin had found it! It had been under his nose all the time. His hand hovered over the spear point, thinking he could feel its energy through the glass as if fire from the ancient volcano still burned inside it. The more he looked at the projectile point, the more beautiful it became: long and lustrous, sharp and deadly. The Clovis artisan—who was Tom and Davy's father—had flintknapped the stone to yield the most strength for its purpose, as if he had seen the point hidden inside all along and just let it out.

This obsidian point was the reason someone not so many years older than himself had left the safety of his camp to walk in a different realm that he could not have been prepared for. At least Kevin had an idea from books and the internet what to expect in Paleolithic times. But his contemporary world was as hostile as the one Tom had left. The Clovis boy had dodged vehicles on the deadly highway at night with headlights hurtling toward him brighter than the furious glint in an ancient bison's eyes. Barbed wire fences with twists sharp as thorns glimmered in the moon's glow, slicing at chest and groin and ankle. Dogs fierce as dire wolves called out to homeowners with guns able to send death faster and farther than any spear. Tom had braved them all in his quest to seek his help to find the point.

Mr. Mason took another map out of the drawer. Kevin saw labels for abandoned mines and Wild West towns, an old train track route and the San Pedro River. Toward the bottom of the map was a circle identified as the Lehner ranch, which Mr. Mason explained was where Ice Age horse and mammoth bones and projectile points had also been discovered. Just north of this was the place where he had found the obsidian point.

"Can we go there?"

"Sure, son. But first we'll have to get your mother's permission."

Kevin's heart sank. Now she would find out he was at the Mason's ranch when he was supposed to be at home.

Mr. Mason made the phone call, explaining to his mother that since Kevin was on his own today (he never mentioned Kevin was already there) and the girls were in town, would she mind if Kevin spent some time with him? When the call ended, he smiled and said, "Good thing you wore jeans today. I'd have hated for you to get saddle burn on those white legs of yours."

Mr. Mason packed the sandwiches Mrs. Mason had left for his lunch, added two canteens of water and headed out to the barn. Gleefully, Kevin followed him, not believing his luck. And a horseback ride, too! He had only ever been on pony rides at fairs, and that was long ago when he was Savannah's age. Mr. Mason threw one of his great Western saddles on Prince and another on Sombra for Kevin. He adjusted Kevin's stirrups.

"Sombra should follow Prince just fine, but if she gets frisky, hold on to the horn. Keep the reins slack, but pull her head up if she tries to eat something along the way. She already has you pegged as a novice rider and may try some tricks. If she does, just give her a few kicks in the ribs to remind her who's boss."

Wyatt and Earp were coming, too. The dogs raced in circles around the barnyard, sending chickens airborne in a cackling cacophony. Mr. Mason led them past Mrs. Mason's garden where green fronds of carrots and onion tops waved good-bye in the gentle morning breeze. As they began their ride through scrubby flat land rabbits bolted across their path, flushed out of cover by the dogs. Prince snorted and tossed his head, but Sombra was unfazed and kept at a steady walk, content to follow the gelding.

Mr. Mason commented, "Out here, with rocks and uneven ground, a good horse has to pay attention where it places its feet." This was all he said for a long while.

They left the Mason Ranch and crossed a paved road and continued on a dirt road parallel to another property. On this ranch, the cattle were gray and had folds of skin under their chins, long droopy ears, and humps on their shoulders.

"Brahmins," Mr. Mason said. "Well, just the cows and castrated males, which we call steers. The bull is in another field."

Kevin was surprised to see houses coming up on his right. They were approaching another small community even further away from where he lived. Mr. Mason called it Hereford. The river was on their left, identifiable by its line of trees. This was the same wide valley the Clovis camp overlooked with its undulating grasses, herds of unfenced camelops and Pleistocene ponies, and the lake that was no longer there. He needed to pay attention if he was going to show Tom and Davy where the projectile point had ended up. He was already dizzy trying to reconcile the view in front of him with the Pleistocene landscape.

Mr. Mason followed the road until it was little more than a path, and suddenly Kevin saw a marker proclaiming the location a national monument, the Lehner Mammoth Kill Site. Unlike Murray Springs, it did not have an interpretative trail. Mr. Mason explained that excavations had stopped decades before. They continued toward the river, which was now very close. A depression in the land opened before them. Prince bounded down, Mr. Mason sitting still in the saddle, looking like a part of the horse instead of a human on top of one. Sombra calmly walked toward the brink after them.

"Hold on to the horn!" Mr. Mason called.

Kevin did. He wobbled from side to side and bounced terribly on his butt, but he did not fall off. At the bottom he gave Mr. Mason a shaky grin.

Mr. Mason dismounted. He helped Kevin off, and then he tethered the horses to a tree to give them some shade. Wyatt and Earp flopped down, panting.

"We'll leave the horses here and go on foot. It's a little rough ahead."

As they proceeded, Kevin could see they were on some sort of trail used by animals. He thought of his trek with Tom and Davy near the river and the warning they had given him.

"Watch out for tapirs!"

Mr. Mason continued walking and did not look back. "How about we watch out for javalina?" he said. "Prehistoric tapirs died out a long time ago in these parts."

"Sure, sure," Kevin said, mentally kicking himself. He didn't want Mr. Mason to think he was crazy.

The sound of the river bubbled up to their ears. Mr. Mason stopped before reaching it, turning to study the stratified wall of the arroyo that ran parallel to it. To Kevin's amazement, he saw the line of the black mat. It was not continuous, being broken in places like the black mat at Murray Springs, but it was there. Mr. Mason pointed to a location directly beneath it.

"The bones were sticking out over here. They hadn't been exposed very long. We'd had a lot of flooding that year, and I just happened to find them first. At the time, it was said to be the best-preserved rib cage of a ground sloth in the Southwest. It's in a museum somewhere now, I think in New York City. They found a jaw with teeth close by, too, but the rest of the skeleton had washed away or been taken by predators. The Clovis point was stuck between two rib bones; the anthropologists speculate just below the heart."

Almost forty years had passed since this discovery, but Kevin could tell Mr. Mason knew where the sloth had died as if he had found it only yesterday. After a few minutes, Mr. Mason said they should return to the horses. The dogs stood up when they saw them and shook off their coats, turned around three times and lay back down. The horses' necks and eyelids drooped in the heat. Mr. Mason pulled the sandwiches out of a saddlebag and they sat down to eat. When he finished his lunch, he lay back with the saddlebag for a pillow, closed his eyes and tilted his hat over his face.

Kevin wondered how long it had taken them to ride here. He peered at Mr. Mason's watch and was surprised to see it was a few minutes past twelve-thirty. He knew his mother and Savannah had left the house at nine, because his mother had turned off a news program on the television that ended at just that time. Kevin reckoned it had taken half an hour to try to fix the bike and get the lift to the ranch, then about forty-five minutes to look at the maps, call his mother and saddle the horses. The ride to reach the Lehner Mammoth Kill Site had taken a little under two hours, and to reach this spot near the river less than ten minutes. When he showed Tom and Davy where the ground sloth had ended up, it would be at the end of a long walk. Then they would have to turn around and head back to camp. He wondered if the effort would be worth it. The spear point had been discovered and was in Mr. Mason's display case; the sloth's bones had been removed, too.

After they returned to the ranch and put the horses away, Kevin followed Mr. Mason into the house. He stared in despair at the obsidian point in the case. He had tried to memorize landmarks so he could find the exact arroyo where the sloth had died, but they were all modern landmarks, such as the little town of Hereford, the Brahman cattle, and paved and dirt roads, all of which would not be there tomorrow. But that night before he fell asleep he remembered something.

TWELVE
KEVIN LEADS THE WAY

THAT EVENING, their father did not call again. Mrs. Sinclair spent some of the next morning before she went to work contacting the person who coordinated information for family members in the unit in which their father served overseas. Yes, they were on a mission. No, no death or serious injury had occurred or she would have been notified. Kevin was concerned about his father, too, but he figured his mother could worry for all of them. On the other hand, he was a little uneasy because Tom had not shown up outside his bedroom window to ask him why he hadn't appeared at the Clovis camp the day before after he had promised to find the spear point, especially with the mammoth hunt coming up.

Mrs. Mason was in the kitchen when they arrived the next morning at Spear Point Ranch.

"Why the long face, Savannah?" she asked.

Savannah moaned. In dramatic style, she put her hands to her chin.

"She went to the dentist yesterday," Kevin explained. "He pulled two teeth."

"Mom didn't tell me I was going to the dentist," Savannah whispered, as if it hurt to talk. "And afterward when we went to the movie my mouth hurt too much to eat popcorn."

"If Mom had told her she was going to the dentist, she would have screamed and cried all the way to Sierra Vista."

"Your mother has enough on her mind, Savannah, to not want to deal with a crybaby. It was a little underhanded, but it got the job done."

Being a rancher's wife, Mrs. Mason was not overly sympathetic about minor complaints. She already had turned back to practical matters, which this morning included baking bread. Savannah recovered quickly from the scolding and drifted over to her. Soon she had her own little loaf and was happily occupied. Mr. Mason walked past Kevin, putting his fingertips to his hat and saying, "Good morning." He continued out the door to his truck and drove away.

Kevin ran over to the glass display case and very gently tried to open the drawer, but it was locked. He wanted to look at the map of the Lehner ranch again because he had noticed something on it yesterday, but he had not paid attention to it. Last night in bed it had popped into his head as ideas sometimes do when you don't expect them. Beneath the circle identifying where the sloth's ribs and the spear point were discovered were degrees of longitude and latitude, just like those that had been on the map identifying where the projectile points had been found at the Murray Springs Clovis Site.

"Melody!" he called, running down the hall to her room where she lay on her bed, thumbs flying across the keyboard on her cell phone.

"I thought we were going to the Clovis camp," she said without looking up.

"If you help me."

"How?"

"I need a copy of a map."

"I thought you knew where to go."

"I do. This is connected. You'll see."

Melody followed him to the living room, where he showed her the map drawer. He watched as she retrieved the key, as he had seen Mr. Mason do. When she unlocked the drawer, the map he needed was still on top. Kevin pointed to where the ribcage had been found.

"Your dad and I went there on Prince and Sombra. I need to go back," he said.

"I know how to get to the Lehner ranch without a map. I grew up here."

"No," Kevin said solemnly. "You think you do, but it won't look the same, and we don't want to get lost."

Melody made a sniff of annoyance, but she looked intrigued. She left the room and a short time later returned with a copy of the map she had made using the family printer. She carefully replaced the original in the drawer, locked the case and put the key in the vase on the bookcase.

"These artifacts are so important to Dad he'll know right away if anything is out of place, even the maps."

"I don't think we need to worry about anything going missing," Kevin said.

"I'll get Savannah ready." But Melody returned a short time later and said, "Mom wants to keep her here. Her face is still a little swollen."

"Does that mean you have to stay, too?"

"Nope. Mom said I was supposed to ask you what you wanted to do." Melody smiled. "So I told her we're going riding!"

Hoping for just such an outcome but not believing it would really happen, Kevin had worn his jeans again. They were a little dirty from the day before and his mother had complained they smelled of horse, but Kevin said no one at the ranch would mind that. They waved goodbye to Savannah and Mrs. Mason and went to the barn.

"Dad said you were a pretty good rider for your first time, but I'm not supposed to ride Prince without Dad around, so we'll both ride Sombra."

Melody saddled her horse with what looked to

Kevin like a blanket with stirrups.

"There's no horn! How do I hold on?"

"You hold on to me, silly."

Melody mounted Sombra and then rode over to the corral where Sid and his dam were watching them with interest.

"Climb on the fence, then swing your leg over Sombra's back," she instructed.

Kevin did as he was told. As they moved away from the corral, his fingers danced around Melody's waist trying to avoid touching her. He had never put his arms around a girl before. They were riding almost bareback, and he felt as if he might slip off at any moment, but after a while, the gentle pacing of the mare gave him some confidence. He relaxed, enjoying the warmth of Sombra's body and the ripple of her muscles moving under his legs, neither of which he had experienced on top of the saddle the day before.

They rode along the highway. Very few cars passed them and when they did, they would slow down and often someone would wave. At one point Melody turned Sombra onto a trail obviously well used by cattle and the loose range horses. They approached the Murray Springs Clovis Site from the southern boundary and reached the interpretive trail. Soon Kevin recognized the twists of the deep gully that gave them access to Tom and Davy's world.

On the edge of the arroyo they had another problem, which was how to get down into it. Melody paced Sombra back and forth until she located the gentlest slope she could find.

"Hold on, Kevin!" she said.

He grasped Melody tightly around the waist, the thought of falling off the horse quickly putting any hesitation out of his mind. Sombra bounced and slid down the dirt face as adroitly as a mountain goat. At the bottom, Kevin told Melody which way to go. The black mat began to fall toward the arroyo floor as they rode up the incline. As the valley opened in front of them, Sombra's ears swiveled forward and her nostrils flared to suck in the cooler, moisture-laden breeze.

"Where are we, Kevin?" Melody whispered.

Kevin felt a little thrill that he had impressed the older girl. He decided to ignore her question. Events would soon take the place of an explanation. He said, "Melody, stop! Don't go any farther. We need to make sure there aren't any bison coming at us." He looked around, but he did not see anything moving on the horizon in any direction. Before them were the oak trees in their small, scattered groves, the lake sparkling in the distance, and the grasses in the valley waving like ocean currents.

"OK," he said. "The coast is clear. Let's go over there." He flipped his right hand toward the hillock, the meeting place with Tom and Davy.

Melody urged Sombra forward. She pranced over

the unfamiliar terrain, tossing her head and flicking her tail like a warhorse, not at all like the docile mare of a few moments ago. Kevin bounced and Melody called to him, "Grip with your legs, too!" which helped a little, but mostly he clung to her like a burr on a sock. He had to lean a little to the side to see in front of them because the top of his head only reached the back of Melody's neck. The grassy mound came into view, but no boys.

Sombra sensed something in front of her. She stopped and would not budge. Under his legs, Kevin could feel her muscles tense. He did not need to be a horse whisperer to know she was about to bolt.

Then he remembered a story from school about the first American indigenous peoples to see sailing ships, and how they had been awestruck and afraid because they could not ever have imagined anything like them. Sombra was not so different from Paleolithic horses, but she was a different color and bigger and there were two humans on top of her. Kevin thought they must be an impressive, bewildering sight to the boys, if indeed they were there. As far as he knew from his brief sojourns to the Clovis camp, the Clovis people did not ride horses; in fact, they ate them. Now he saw something ahead in a tangle of low, thick bushes. It was either the brothers in hiding or a predator. He gambled it was the boys.

"It's Kevin and a friend! Come out if you can hear me!"

Tom and Davy appeared. Tom carried his spear, raised as if to send it flying.

"Cavemen!" Melody said. "How much did you pay them to come here?"

"They were here a long time before we were. Help me down."

Sombra calmed enough to allow Melody to help Kevin slide off. He ran toward the brothers.

"I found it! I found your father's spear point!"

They looked expectantly at him as if he was about to pull it out of his pocket.

"No, no. I don't have it, but I know where it was."

"You don't have it?" Davy asked.

Kevin sputtered. He did not know how to explain to Davy there was no way he could bring the obsidian point from the Mason ranch to the Clovis camp. Mr. Mason would surely notice it was gone.

Melody had dismounted. She approached them, leading Sombra.

"Stop waving that spear around! You're spooking my horse."

Davy was staring at Sombra and Tom was staring at Melody. Kevin had not foreseen the possibility that Tom might be attracted to Melody.

"They're a little scruffy, aren't they," she said, "almost as if they need a good scrubbing and a hair-cut. The clothes are pretty cool though—animal skins and headbands."

Indeed, Kevin noticed the brothers wore more

than their usual plain loincloths. These garments were sewn together, covered their chests and shoulders, and were decorated with beads made from shells, acorns and a few small stones.

"The feathers on the spear are a nice touch, too."

Davy, who appeared to have understood almost everything Melody had said, asked, "What's scruffy?"

Kevin shot a warning glance at Melody and replied, "It means you look like mighty hunters!"

Davy beamed.

"What's with the new outfits?" Kevin asked.

"Our father's sister and relatives from her husband's clan have arrived. We dress in respect for their visit and to show how prosperous we are. It is also to get the attention of the spirit gods so they will notice us and look favorably on our new mammoth hunters!"

"Sure," Kevin said, a little uncomfortable at the mention of supernatural forces, which appeared to be very strong around here or how could he cross boundaries thirteen thousand years apart? Better not to dwell on that now.

"These actors are really good," Melody said. "I can't understand what they're babbling, but sometimes a word or two pops into my brain and I know what it means. Isn't that weird?"

It was obvious Melody was still unconvinced they were not in their own world.

"Dad says there is a place called Government

Draw at Lewis Springs," she said. "It's somewhere near here. Anthropologists say it's supposed to have some of the same vegetation as in Paleolithic times. The arroyo must have led us into it. You're very clever, Kevin, to pull all this together just to entertain me!"

"I've never heard of Government Draw," Kevin said. What he needed now was a camelops or two or a herd of Pleistocene horses to persuade Melody this was not the twenty-first century.

"I want to see where the spear point *was*," Tom said sorrowfully.

Kevin heard the struggle of coming to terms with the obsidian point being lost forever in the Clovis boy's words. He took the map and a compass out of his pocket. He had learned how to use a compass in Boy Scouts in an orienteering class; his father, in fact, had taught it. He had been so proud to see his dad in uniform in front of his troop. Afterwards, the boys had shown Kevin a lot of respect for the next couple of meetings, and it had even overflowed onto the schoolyard after lunch period for more than a week.

He spread the map on the ground and placed the compass on top of it. Finding Point A, which was where they were near the Murray Springs site, he aligned the edge of the compass and the directional lines toward Point B, where the ground sloth had died. Rotating the map and compass until the red arrow pointed north—and double-checking that it was north, not south in the opposite direction, which was a mistake some beginners made—he came up with a plan. The travel arrow pointed in the direction he initially assumed they should go, but because they were starting out further east than he had yesterday with Mr. Mason, he wanted to make doubly sure due to the absence of modern-day landmarks.

"This way!" he announced, thinking Lewis and Clark must have experienced the same excitement setting out on their search for the Northwest Passage. He walked purposefully through the almost waist-high grass, Tom and Davy beside him. Melody on Sombra brought up the rear.

In a little while, it became apparent that Tom and Davy were walking faster than he was. Remembering that the trip on horseback to the gully near the river yesterday had taken almost two hours, Kevin had esti-mated at least the same or more today, but because the boys covered the ground with long, loping strides, and even Sombra had picked up her pace, they should make it in less time. Kevin began to fall behind. He wondered if anyone would think badly of him if he asked Melody for a ride. He finally stopped altogether to fake a look at the compass and catch his breath.

"Why don't you get on Sombra with me?" Melody said, pulling the mare to a halt. "Then you can look at the compass while we keep going."

The boys had stopped, too, and were petting the horse. When Kevin approached, they linked arms and boosted him up. He took his bearings again and directed Melody a couple of degrees to the west. He had to adjust further when they approached the lake to go around it. Fortunately, it was not a very big lake.

"I don't remember a lake here," Melody said. "I haven't seen any cows or fences or roads since we came out of the arroyo. And your actors must be on the track team in school because they sure can move along."

"They aren't actors, Melody." Her long chestnut braid flopped on her back with the rhythm of the horse's gait, and Kevin had a wicked desire to pull it.

One of the principles Kevin remembered from his dad's class was to identify spots on the map as a way to ensure you were headed where you wanted to go, but this wasn't possible on Mr. Mason's modern day map. He called an adjustment to the left as they approached the river, which was now identifiable by a green ribbon of cottonwoods and willows. As they continued he looked around for the arroyo where Mr. Mason had found the sloth the day before, but he did not see it. In fact, he did not see anything resembling a gully or draw, as they were sometimes called. Only a little tributary of the river twinkling in the sunlight sliced the big plain not far away.

Sombra stopped suddenly and the boys stopped, too, questions in their eyes. The horse stamped a hoof and snorted, looking toward the river. Then she arced her head around to look at Melody.

"What's she doing?" Kevin asked.

"She's telling me she wants to stay here. Like she's been here before or something."

"Yes!"

Kevin slid off Sombra's back and headed toward the tributary, the brothers trotting by his side. Tom's spear skimmed the grass like a low-flying eagle.

"Now, don't be disappointed that it's not here," Kevin began. "I was here yesterday and it wasn't—"

"I see something!" Tom called, jumping up and down. He pointed to the further bank. In a moment he was wading through the shallow water. Davy plunged in after his brother. Kevin began to follow, wanting to see what Tom had glimpsed hidden in the stream's vegetation. He stopped short when he felt as if a hand had been placed on his shoulder. For a crazy second, he thought it might be the boys' father. If you could go back 13,000 years in time, could you not go back 13,000 years plus two, back before the tragedy happened, and so avoid it altogether? Just as quickly he realized no one was next to him. He looked around, but all he saw was Melody walking toward him and Sombra grazing in the background.

Tom was parting the reeds. Kevin saw bones of an animal with remnants of brown fur attached. Some bones were missing, but the ribcage remained. A bear-like skull was next to it, as if the huge animal had lain down in its last agony before its final sleep. It was the skeleton of the ground sloth, and it had not been there the day before.

THIRTEEN

THE OBSIDIAN POINT

MELODY SAT down by Kevin on the streambank. They dangled their legs over the water while Ice Age gnats and dragonflies buzzed around their heads as they watched Tom thrust his hand through the rib cage.

"What's he doing?" Melody asked.

Suddenly the Paleo-Indian boy leaped back from the carcass.

"Eye-ee-ah!" he roared, so loudly that Sombra jerked her head up and whinnied. Tom began to dance with joy, kicking up great sprays of water. Davy joined him, whooping and hollering. Some waterfowl Kevin had not noticed before rose up and circled overhead, honking repeatedly at the disturbance. The brothers in their exuberance began scooping water at each other, then on him and Melody, Tom with one hand only because in the other he was holding something aloft between thumb and forefinger.

Finally, the boys crawled up the bank and threw themselves down beside Kevin and Melody, who was wet but amused.

"What did you find?" she asked peering at Tom's hand. "Oh my God, Kevin, it's Dad's obsidian projectile point! Did you put it in your pocket while I was copying the map?"

"Of course not! I'm sure the spear point will be there just as it was this morning," he said, but it really was just bluster. He had no idea how the obsidian point had turned up here. He challenged, "How do you know it's the same as your Dad's?"

"I grew up with the obsidian point in the glass case. I can tell you the pattern of each flute on it and on the others, too. Kevin, this is serious. We've got to get that projectile point back before Dad notices it's missing. This was a fun game, even to planting the skeleton of a – by the way what was that?"

"A ground sloth."

"Yeah, sure. A giant ground sloth."

"No, it's just a ground sloth. The giant variety live further north."

"Kevin, cut it out! You were very clever to plant some cow bones at the edge of a stream in somebody's pasture, but I've got to take this home." She made a motion to take the spear point out of Tom's fingers, but he deftly rolled over and stood up.

"Sharp," he said, turning and beginning to walk away. Davy hurried to catch up with his brother, calling back to them, "It's time to return to camp." Kevin wondered how much Davy had understood of their conversation.

Melody took Sombra's reins and led the horse until they came to a fallen tree that served as a mounting block. The boys were far ahead now.

"You couldn't have taken it, Kevin," she said apologetically as she pulled him up behind her. "I was with you the entire time we were in the living room except when I went to copy the map. All five projectile points were in the case when I locked it up. I think. It really can't be the same projectile point," she said, struggling to convince herself. "But I must say it's an awfully good likeness."

Melody put her heels to Sombra and the horse broke into a canter. In no time they were together again. Davy dropped away from his brother to walk next to the horse and looked up at Kevin with eloquent eyes. Kevin understood what he wanted.

"Melody," he said. "Can you give Davy a ride?"

"If someone can help him up," she said, stopping the horse.

Kevin slid off. Tom came over and handed his spear to Kevin while he swung Davy behind Melody. Kevin had never held a spear; in fact, he had never held a weapon, except once his Dad's rifle. Another year, his parents said, and then he could learn to shoot. He felt an awesome sense of power holding the spear, which seemed a natural extension of his body, almost as if his blood pulsed through it, too, as sap had once done through the shaft. He wanted desperately to make it fly.

Tom was studying him.

"It's too late today, but come back tomorrow and we'll teach you how to throw it," he said, reaching for the spear.

As Sombra moved forward, Kevin called up to Davy, "You have to grab on to Melody or you might fall off."

Kevin knew Davy would be reluctant to hold on to her. He had noticed in his brief time in the camp that Clovis people were not big on hugs or other physical signs of affection. Tom and Davy had never slipped an arm over his shoulder like a Greek philosopher to express familiarity or clapped him on the back like a football player in acknowledgment of a terrific play, and no one had offered to shake his hand when he was introduced. Somewhere Kevin had read that shaking a person's hand developed out of a need to find out if a fellow was hiding a weapon in it, but that had come much later in history.

"Davy told me the spear point belongs to Melody's father in your world," Tom said as they walked.

"I think she was trying to make sense of why it was here, not locked in the glass case in the living-room where her father keeps it at the ranch house." Kevin could tell he had thrown out too much information about present-day human life, but it seemed to him that Tom was getting better at detecting the important points of their conversations, just as he was with him.

"Which world do you think it belongs to?"

Kevin shook his head. He did not have an answer. He was wondering if something could be in two places at once. He did not think so. He thought to himself, *I'll know this afternoon when we get back if it's missing from the glass case.*

"What will you do, Ke'on, if the spear point is not there and they accuse you of taking it? We have consequences for those who take other's possessions without permission."

"We do, too."

Tom began to speak again, but in choppy sentences as if he was trying to work out how he felt and what he should do. He said he was confused over loyalty to his new friend, who had done what he requested and found what he most desired. Now Ke'on might suffer for having succeeded in doing so. Passionately, Tom explained he wanted to keep his father's most valued piece, not only for its exquisite craftsmanship but also for its deadly nature, saying that the spear point possessed a life force powerful enough to attract and kill game. Kevin was skeptical that the obsidian point held a magical soul like a genie in a bottle, but if what Tom believed made his eye more focused, his wrist and arm a little steadier, and gave him the ability to concentrate so that nothing existed but him and the target, who was he to say it was wrong?

Suddenly they heard a cry from Davy.

"Over there, To'meh! I see them!"

Everyone looked in the direction where he was wildly waving his hand.

"They're huge," Melody called from her vantage point on top of the horse. "I think they're elephants."

Davy said something to Tom, but Kevin had already guessed.

"Those aren't elephants, Melody," he said. "Those are mammoths."

"Oh Kevin, don't be ridiculous! It's a herd of elephants on the Three Bar O Ranch. Dad told us Mr. Lynch was going in for raising exotic animals, like for big game safaris for tourists. You wouldn't hunt the elephants, of course, but they would be a nice touch, as if you really were in Africa."

Tom was gleeful at the news of the appearance of the animals. "We'll have the hunt soon. The herds come to the waterhole near the camp and stay there for a few days at a time." He began to skip, run and feint with his spear as if he was approaching one of the giant creatures in his imagination.

"Well, I think you might be right that they're mammoths," Melody continued. "They have high foreheads, not at all flat like the kind of elephant we know, and their ears are small, not big and floppy.

And goodness, some of them have long tusks that curve toward each other."

Kevin wondered if she was finally admitting they really were back in prehistoric times.

But then she added, "And they're covered in shaggy brown hair, even on their faces."

Kevin sighed. She was pulling his leg. She was describing the woolly mammoths that had roamed in northern latitudes, not Columbian mammoths, and she knew the difference because Mr. Mason had explained this to them a couple of days before when they had stopped at the interpretive sign on the Murray Springs Clovis Site trail.

A short time later they reached the grassy mound. The sun shone directly over their heads in a bright blue sky. When he heard his stomach rumble, Kevin speculated it was close to lunchtime. Davy slipped off Sombra, and he and Tom offered their hands so Kevin could get on.

"Tomorrow!" Tom called, lifting his spear. He gave Melody a look that even Kevin could interpret, and the brothers ran off.

"I think Tom wants you to come again, too," he said.

"He's very nice for a caveman," Melody replied as she turned Sombra in the direction of the arroyo. "And Davy is a lot like you—totally irritating, but he seems like a good enough kid. He told me all about the Clovis camp. He must have done a lot of research for his part."

"But you saw the mammoths?" Kevin said hopefully. After all, most people thought of woolly mammoths when they did think of mammoths.

"I was only playing my role in your grand scheme. There were some big and lumpy animals out there, but I couldn't see them clearly. Sometimes when I'm riding on the ranch Dad will point out javalina or antelope and I can't see them very well, either. Mom says I'll need glasses before I take the test for my driver's license."

They did not talk again until they had gone down the wash and up the other side. As they headed south through the scrubby brush toward the highway, Kevin asked, "What time is it, Melody?"

"That's a good question. I swear, Kevin, it was high noon just a minute ago." She pointed toward the west and said, "Now I'd say it is much later. It's like time sped up." She pulled out her cell phone. "It's four thirty-five in the afternoon!"

Although he could not see her face, he could feel the tension in Melody's body where he gripped her around the waist. She must be trying to process this information, which he found very disturbing, too. He thought she was finally going to have to admit "there" and "here" were two different places. But one question was on both their minds.

"Kevin, we've got to see if the obsidian projectile point is in the case!"

Once they reached the highway, a number of cars and trucks passed them as if going home from work. When they turned into the Mason's driveway, Sombra broke into a trot. Every horse moves faster on its way toward the barn than away from it, especially at feeding time. As soon as she reached it, Kevin and Melody were off in a flash and running into the house.

FOURTEEN

IT CERTAINLY IS A CONUNDRUM

WHAT MET their eyes was a mess in the living room, which had been in good order when they left the house that morning.

The carpet between the sofas had been rolled up and lay like a colorful sausage on top of one of them. On the other sofa, a table lamp and a jumble of knick-knacks, books and magazines had been strewn. The remainder of the furniture was set at odd angles. Nothing was in its right place. Even the floor-length curtains had been lifted and draped over their rods as if someone wanted to make sure nothing was hidden beneath them. The dogs prowled around the room, sniffing at scents not uncovered for years. Minute particles like fairy dust glittered in the remaining light slanting through the windows, making Kevin's eyes itch. They looked to the right of the fireplace. The glass case on its special stand was not there.

"We've been found out, Kevin," Melody said. "They've searched the room for the missing projectile point."

Melody's face had gone very pale and her eyes were huge like saucers. Kevin felt terrible. He had convinced her to help him, and now he had gotten her in trouble. She knew where the key to the glass case was kept, so if no one else in the house admitted to taking the projectile point, she would be the obvious culprit, even though all she had done was copy the map. They had been so focused on the map the fact that neither of them could remember if the obsidian projectile point was in the case when they left was alarming. What was it Mrs. Bowersock often quoted to him and Savannah when they were tempted to behave badly? It had something to do with spiders, but really it did not. Standing there looking at the chaos in the living room, he remembered: "Oh what a tangled web we weave when first we practice to deceive!" Now he understood what it meant.

Mrs. Mason strode into the room, calling out, "Where on earth have you two been?" Then she saw the dogs. "Wyatt! Earp! Get out of here this instant!" As they bolted from the living room she said, "Watch where you step. We had the grout redone today and it's still drying. The contractor will be back tomorrow to seal it. Place your feet on the stones, not on the lines between them. And come into the kitchen out of this dust."

Kevin glanced at Melody, whose eyes had receded to normal, although he could see a nerve twitch under the one closest to him. Mrs. Mason had not mentioned the projectile point.

"You need to find the glass case!" he whispered to Melody.

She sneezed and answered, "I've got to take care of Sombra."

Kevin waited in the kitchen for Melody to come back, but she had chores to do and did not return. A fan had been strategically placed to blow the powdery substance produced by the grout back into the living room.

"It'll be a couple of days before this stuff settles," Mrs. Mason said, reaching for her truck keys. "Your mother has already been here to pick up Savannah. I'll run you home."

On the ride to his house Mrs. Mason said, "I think you're old enough to hear this, although your mother disagrees. Your dad's unit is still in the field. It's been a longer and more dangerous mission than usual. Due to security reasons, no one is allowed to know where they are or what they're doing. Right now, not knowing is the worst of it, isn't it? So I expect you to be the man of the house. That means being respectful and helpful to your mother and kind to your sister— no fights over silly things—until we know about your dad. Understood?"

"Yes, ma'am," Kevin said.

As they pulled into the driveway, Mrs. Mason added, "We'll see you and Savannah tomorrow. I'm sure you can find something to do that doesn't involve playing in the living room."

The house was quiet. No lights were on, but there was a glow in the kitchen's western-facing window; through it, he saw the orb of the sun touching the tips of the Huachuca Mountains, under which the fort was located. His mother sat at the kitchen table looking out of the window. When he came closer he saw she had her glasses on; golden points of light reflected on each lens. She only wore her glasses if she had been crying and had to remove her contacts. He thought that at this very moment the boys might be showing the spear point to their mother, and he wondered if she would cry, too, thinking of their father.

"Kevin," she said, "sit down. I've something to tell you. I told Mrs. Mason I wouldn't, but she said I should, and I think she is right."

His mother repeated what Mrs. Mason had said. She did not need to add they were to keep this from Savannah.

"Your sister's had dinner and I put her to bed. I'll get you something."

"I can make myself a sandwich, Mom."

"Thank you, son," his mother said.

Kevin went to the refrigerator and pretended to study its contents, blinded by the tears swelling under his eyelids. The sun dropped behind the mountains.

When he finally shut the refrigerator door, the kitchen was dark. He took the opportunity to draw the back of his hand across his face where it was wet. He was not hungry, after all.

Before he went to bed, he studied his clock. It was the old-fashioned type with a minute hand. He watched the hand chip away a full sixty seconds before he believed the passage of time was as it should be, in the here and now. He noted the time as he turned out his light. In the morning a full eight hours had passed, the usual time he spent in bed each night. He was surprised at his relief that time had not skipped forward again.

IF ANYONE COULD ACHIEVE something simply by putting her mind to it, it was Mrs. Mason. Now she had turned her energies to restoring the living room floor in the old ranch house. She attacked it with gusto as if it had worn away just to irritate her and distract her from more important things, such as her laying hens and vegetable garden. When they arrived the next morning, she was standing over two workmen who knelt at her feet and were painting a foul-smelling substance over the newly patched grout to seal it from dirt and moisture.

Melody met Kevin with a look on her face that indicated she knew something about the projectile point. Savannah skipped gaily past them toward Melody's room, her bag of dolls in tow.

"I'll be right there," Melody called. She dragged Kevin down the hall and through a door that had been shut the entire time he had been in the house.

"This is my brother's room," she said. "My parents close the door to keep the dust off the trophies."

She pointed to shelves a few feet down from the ceiling that went around the bedroom on which awards were displayed. Kevin recognized some for sports, others for 4-H, and additional ones for Boy Scouts and Rotary. Then in a corner of the room he saw a piece of furniture covered by a thick blanket of the heavy variety used to move delicate furniture. On it was the logo "Ace Tile and Grout."

"The workers must have moved the display case, because this blanket belongs to them. If Mom or Dad had done it, they would have noticed the projectile point was missing."

Kevin had to see for himself. He carefully lifted up an edge of the blanket. Where the obsidian point should have been was empty.

"Come on, Kevin," Melody whispered urgently. "We have to get out of here before Mom gets suspicious."

At that moment, Mrs. Mason walked into the bedroom.

"What are you two doing in here?"

Kevin slowly lowered the edge of the contractor's blanket and turned around.

Melody said brightly, "I was showing Brad's trophies to Kevin."

"Oh, yes," Mrs. Mason replied, looking up at the shelves. "Isn't this impressive? Brad made a pact with himself that he'd fill all four walls with awards before he went off to college. And he did!"

"Mel-o-dee," they heard Savannah call, stretching out each syllable like a musical note. Melody and Kevin excused themselves and left the room. Mrs. Mason shut the door behind them and headed toward the kitchen.

In Melody's bedroom they made plans. Mrs. Mason had made it clear to Melody she would be responsible for Savannah today, unlike yesterday. Melody wanted to go back where they had been to retrieve the obsidian projectile point, and Kevin wanted to learn to throw a spear. They decided on a picnic lunch in case time got out of control again and they grew hungry. Melody told Savannah to pack a few dolls—not the entire collection—to entertain herself if she got bored. She gave her what had been her own pink backpack as a little girl to put them in, and then they trooped out to the kitchen to make sandwiches and add juice boxes and cookies. The contractors were busy in the living room when they left the house.

Melody chose to put her roping saddle on Sombra.

Savannah would ride in front between her and the horn, and Kevin would ride behind the cantle, the raised back lip of the seat. The extra weight would hardly slow Sombra down because the three of them together weighed as much as a good-sized man, and Sombra had no problem carrying Mr. Packer from the next ranch over but one, and he had a stomach that draped over his belt like a sack of flour.

Mr. Mason was working on his tractor and came up to them to check that the saddle's girth was snug.

"Where are you off to?"

Melody pointed in the direction of the Murray Springs Clovis Site, but it was so vague a wave of her hand that it could have been anywhere going east.

"Say, Dad," she said, suddenly remembering. "Does Mr. Lynch have elephants?"

"Not that I'm aware of. He has a few giraffes, a couple of ibexes and a pair of zebras. Oh, and some camels, too. I'd think everyone in the county would know if he had elephants."

Kevin poked Melody, who in turn made an attempt to elbow him, but he knew it was coming and leaned back.

"No barrel racing with that little girl in front," Mr. Mason said.

"No, Dad," Melody drawled, rolling her eyes.

Mr. Mason smiled at them and patted Sombra on the rump.

"Have a good time."

Sombra walked sedately down the driveway to the road as if she knew she had a precious cargo on board. Savannah clutched the horn, her small hands barely reaching around it. Her legs rested on Melody's pink backpack on one side and on Kevin's navy blue one containing their lunch on the other, conveniently sparing her the wide straddle of the big saddle.

A brisk wind blew cotton clouds across an azure sky. It was warm enough to dress in short sleeves, but a change was coming soon, Kevin had heard his mother say. Maybe a thunderstorm, traveling up from Mexico. Right now he could not imagine any of this for the future. He could only concentrate on where they were going in the past.

Twenty minutes later, they entered the archeological dig and located the arroyo with the black mat.

"OK, Kevin," Melody said. "Hold on tight to me because I need to hold onto Savannah when Sombra jumps down. Ready, set, go!"

As soon as Sombra reached the solid floor of the gully, Melody turned her toward the entrance to the Paleolithic valley. In no time, they were staring out at the wide expanse of lush grasses, clusters of oak trees and the lake.

"This is somewhere else. Why are we here?" Savannah asked. She turned her head toward the mountains where she said she saw dinosaurs. The mountains were much closer now. "I want to go home."

Kevin wondered if she really had seen dinosaurs, just as he saw Clovis people. A shiver went through him.

Not far away, a herd of about a dozen adult and juvenile animals ambled toward them. He had seen them on his second visit to the valley.

"Camels!" Melody said triumphantly. "Dad said there were camels on Mr. Lynch's ranch!"

"These are camelops," Kevin corrected her. He conceded the camelops did look an awful lot like the camels he had seen in a zoo, even to having the flat, padded bottoms of their feet. What he was not prepared for was their size, because the first time he had seen them they had been far away. The camelops were much larger than their modern cousins. Melody's cowboy hat was about even with the shoulders of the largest animals, and their heads were attached to long necks that rose a good couple of feet from there. They seemed peaceful creatures as they looked down with liquid brown eyes under thick eyelashes at the horse and children. They wove around Sombra on elongated, muscular legs, leaving little doubt they could cover long distances and quickly, too. Kevin almost reached out to pat one, but he thought better of it. They had large teeth for grinding vegetation, and who knew if a human arm might be tempting to nip if one was annoyed?

"These are the biggest camels I've ever seen," Melody said. "I wonder what Mr. Lynch is feeding them."

"When will you give up?" Kevin insisted. "We've gone back in time. You just have to accept it. You can't explain the missing projectile point, or how it appeared here, can you?"

"It certainly is a conundrum," she admitted.

"What's that?" Savannah asked.

"A puzzle."

"I want to go home," Savannah wailed again. One of the camelops sniffed her hair, knocking her hat off.

"We'll go home after we go to the Clovis camp," Kevin replied.

FIFTEEN

CAN YOU SAY ATLATL?

THEY LEFT Savannah's hat where it had fallen into a bramble bush. No one wanted to dismount where it would be difficult to get back on, and what if the camelops herd came back? They did appear to be curious beasts.

The boys were not at the grassy mound. Kevin was disappointed, but he remembered their aunt was visiting and besides, the brothers could not spend all day lounging around if the tribe was getting ready for the mammoth hunt. They continued on, and a short time later the rounded shapes of the houses came into view. He saw Rescalispel's dwelling with its ivory tusks decorating the entrance and wondered if Slats was inside.

Past and future time appeared synchronized today. The atmosphere still had the freshness associated with morning, and the sun was still climbing toward its zenith. The Clovis people were employed in various occupations, much as they had been when Kevin had first seen them. Just as they had done then, they paused in their activities and stared. This time, however, they did not approach them. Kevin thought perhaps it was Sombra with the three of them astride, an incomprehensible combination of humans and horse that astounded them, just as it had Tom and Davy. Some of the men reached for their spears, and Kevin saw a few grab what looked like clubs. The women laboring in housekeeping duties joined the crowd for safety and caught the hands of small children. Beyond them, Kevin saw Rescalispel with his long hair, loincloth and necklaces. The man was staring not at him, Melody, or the horse, but at Savannah.

"Tom! Davy!" Kevin called uneasily, not seeing the brothers.

Suddenly out of one of the houses shot a ball of tan fur with a head, short legs and a tail.

"Mitzi!" Savannah cried, wiggling to be let down.

The crowd began to mutter and Kevin heard exclamations of surprise or fear. This was not the warm welcome he had experienced previously and expected. He had an urgent desire to tell Melody to turn the horse around and go back. He would make up a story why the projectile point was missing, maybe even smash the glass to make them think he had stolen it. He would be disgraced and punished, but that seemed a better plan than putting his little sister and Melody in danger. He felt responsibility settle on his shoulders like one of the circlets of tails from unidentifiable beasts that some of the men wore around their necks. Trophies came in all forms, not just like those that rimmed Brad's bedroom walls.

"Kevin," Melody whispered. "What did you get us into?"

At that moment, to his great relief, Kevin saw Tom and Davy emerge from the house from which Mitzi had come. A tall woman, taller than any of the other women and even some of the men, too, followed them. She must be the aunt, he decided, elder sister of Tom and Davy's father. Her face was proud and stern, and it was obvious she was in charge because people parted to make way for her; even Rescalispel took a few steps back. Her black hair was twisted on top of her head, and from this topknot a crown of ringlets tumbled out. Her flowing gown was sewn from the most supple of animal skins and had a border of fur like a rabbit's. She wore several necklaces, which by now Kevin recognized as symbols of wealth and power; from one dangled a magnificent pink seashell. She had the longer face, prominent inward-angled cheekbones, wide-set eyes and broader nose of the Clovis people. She looked queenly and exotic, and Kevin had the curious urge to bow, which would have been an impossible stunt on top of the horse as he peered around Melody, but he managed to nod his head. The woman acknowledged this with a slight raise of an eyebrow.

Savannah had not paid any attention to the crowd or the elegant woman, but only to Mitzi, who continued to jump around Sombra's hocks trying to reach her. Finally, she could not bear it. She lifted a leg over the saddle horn and started to slip to the ground. Melody was quick to catch her wrists and lower her down, the patient horse not moving a muscle even though Melody had let go of the reins.

"I have to get off, too!" Kevin said.

Melody took a boot out of its stirrup and indicated he was to put his shoe in it to help him dismount. He grabbed her leg on the way down, which was a little embarrassing, and bruised his elbow on a saddle buckle. As soon as he was on the ground, he put his arms around Savannah, who was now holding Mitzi. The aunt had stopped a few feet away, no longer looking at him but at Savannah, as was everyone else. She said something, her Clovis voice deep and mellifluous with occasional trills and here and there a guttural sound. Davy scooted up to translate.

"My father's sister gives you greeting. She asks you to address her by her name, Irtyshi. You are welcome here because you found the spear point belonging to her brother. We will honor you by a tale told around the hearth fires for as many years as there are stars in the sky. But my aunt would like to know why you brought this child to us today. She wonders if she is an offering of your good will."

"She's my sister, Savannah, and she's with us today because Melody is baby—, uh, Melody is— An offering?"

Davy was a little confused about this, too, but when he presented Kevin's question to his aunt and received a reply, he turned back to Kevin with a solemn face.

"The spirit world is speaking. Your sister will bring prosperity to our tribe. Mammoths and bison will appear when we are hungry, so we will no longer have to make great journeys to find them. Dire wolves and long-toothed cats will cease to snatch our babies because the great beasts will be plentiful and satisfy the hunger of all. We will fashion garments from their hides and tools from their bones and …"

Davy went on in a rather pompous voice, but Kevin's attention caught on something his friend had said that made sense to him. He remembered reading that humans were thought to play a role in the great extinctions of the Ice Age by preying on the same animals that fed their predators. The Clovis people hunted the females and young because they were the easiest to bring down, and when they did this, they removed them from reproducing. A shift to a more arid climate was reducing the abundance of vegetation for the herbivores and leading to the drying up of cienegas and lakes, such as the one that no longer existed near Murray Springs. Then he thought he heard his sister's name, and his attention returned to Davy.

"S'anna," Davy said, like Tom, having trouble pronouncing his v's, "comes to us from the land where the sun is born each day. Legend tells us fair-haired, blued-eyed people dwell there." As if to confirm this, Savannah's blonde hair tossed in the breeze as delicate and weightless as dandelion fluff, and her blue eyes had opened wide to take in the assembly of people in front of her. Davy continued in rather grand style, "Her skin is pink and white like seashells, so she is sister, too, to fish, which bring good luck to everyone and fertility to women." This last Davy added without a blush. He concluded in a tone that even arrested Melody's attention, which had obviously drifted because it was apparent she understood only a few words, by announcing: "Today, my people have met the daughter of the First Person to walk this land!"

Suddenly, there was a cry like a seagull's, but no bird was in sight; however, a stab of shadow crossed the sun. A man who had once traveled to the ocean exclaimed, "The Spirit Girl has brought this totem with her. I know the seabird's call!" The crowd murmured in excitement, but it was a friendly noise now. The prospect of well-being was making the tribe festive.

Someone brought out a drum. An old man, whom

Davy called the Storyteller, began to chant in time to the slow beat. He told the legend of a place called Soldorador, which Davy whispered meant "the land of sun worshipers." The Storyteller called out this tale from memory, keeping the past alive in these prehistoric times as he stood in the center of the camp leaning on a staff near a cooking pit where fat root tubers smoldered in hot ash embers, producing a satisfying smell like baked potatoes. The Clovis people went back to work while listening to the Storyteller, respectful and industrious at the same time, now and then casting an eye on Savannah.

Kevin was impressed by how easily the clans accepted his sister as coming from the dominion of spirits. Davy explained spirits inhabit everybody, and one only had to find the right time and place to express itself, as Savannah's was doing now. The attitude of the Clovis people was something like this: "Well, of course she should appear to us, it is foretold!" Kevin giggled because Savannah was his sister, not some supernatural phenomenon.

"What's so funny?" Melody asked.

Before he could answer, Irtyshi stepped forward and indicated that Savannah was to come with her. Savannah did not hesitate, which surprised Kevin because they had always been told to be wary of strangers, but what could be better in an awkward situation than to accept the protection of the most powerful person present? They went off to the center of the village, Savannah's pale hand tucked into the lady's dusky palm, the two appearing very companionable although they had just met. The boys' aunt had begun a conversation. Savannah looked at Irtyshi as if she understood most of what the lady said. Kevin guessed his sister also had the gift to communicate with the Paleo-Indian people. Mitzi trotted after them. They went not to the women's house, but to another. It was newly constructed and better built than the others as he could see by the tightness of its lashed tree-limb structure and the density of its thatch stuffing. They disappeared inside. Berul followed with Tom and Davy's toddler sister, plus two girls and a boy who resembled Irtyshi. Kevin thought they must be her children. A couple of sturdy-looking men squatted outside, leaving no doubt they were bodyguards.

Kevin looked around for Tom, but his glance fell instead on Rescalispel and Slats. Rescalispel wore the fuming expression of someone who is being ignored, reminding Kevin why Irtyshi had come, which was to serve as referee to the succession of her birth clan. This was serious business.

Tom approached them, the spear with the obsidian tip on a dart clutched in his right hand. Melody eyed the projectile point. Kevin could tell by the way she looked at it she was determined to get it back. He thought she might even grab the spear, jump on Sombra and gallop into the future. In the end, she turned her attention to observing the camp, her face reflecting her interest in what was going on. She looked at the bison processing site, now abandoned except for piles of long, pale horns stacked alongside. Nearby were the drying racks with meat lined up like fringes on a cowgirl's skirt, protected from birds by a net of woven plant fibers. In front of them the houses and hearths encircled the Storyteller, who was still droning away, and beyond that was the flat land dotted with wild melons and gourds toward which the young men of the village and a few elders were walking.

"Time for spear practice!" Tom said.

As they walked through the Clovis camp, the boy who Kevin thought might be Irtyshi's son, and therefore Tom and Davy's cousin, emerged from the house and came toward them. He looked a little younger than Tom, but not by much. His face had the sharper angles of his mother, and he was tall, like she was. His eyes resembled Tom's with the same irresistible intensity, and he had Davy's friendly smile. He said something to Tom, who turned to Davy, who turned to Kevin.

"Chukotka is going with you. My aunt requests Melody to join her. Savannah has asked that Melody bring her dolls with her. I am to go to my aunt and mother, too. I don't know why I can't come with you," he complained to Tom.

"You are destined to become a flintknapper, not a

hunter," he said, making the job sound less important than it really was, as if there were more glory in taking down a mammoth than providing the weapon to do it. "You have the skill already, little brother," he added more kindly. "You will follow in our father's footsteps."

Tom's last words seemed some comfort to Davy. He obediently went to the house with Melody, who had tied Sombra to a tree and already returned with the pink backpack. They passed inside between the guards, disappearing from the curious eyes of the rest of the people. The Storyteller continued the legend of Soldorador, and occasionally someone would nod and point to Irtyshi's house to mark his words. Kevin wondered if the tale had a happy ending.

He followed Tom and Chukotka through the camp to where the boys and men were practicing spear throwing. The ground was level for about the length of a basketball court, and then it rose to small hillocks on which targets had been positioned. Tom explained these were placed at different heights depending on the beasts they were pursuing. Today the boys were practicing for mammoth and their aim had to be higher than for bison.

"Go for the heart or a lung," Tom said. "A quick and efficient death is an honor to both hunter and beast."

A man stepped up to them, stocky as a drill sergeant and looking just as purposeful. His name was a tongue twister and slipped out of Kevin's mind as soon as they were introduced. He accepted Kevin's presence as if he had been born in the tribe, which made Kevin want to perform his best for him.

The elder carried one of the spear-throwing devices Kevin had noticed before, and which he now knew was called an atlatl. It was designed to extend the arm like an extra joint, making it possible to throw farther with more force. This one was about two feet long. On one end was a hook made of carved antler, and on the other was a smooth flat area for a handhold around which a thin braid of tendon had been twisted for a grip.

Tom explained that the deadly sharp spear points, such as the obsidian point, were kept for hunting, not practice. He laid his precious weapon to the side. Then he picked up a hollow, lightweight spear made of willow and into this inserted a smaller shaft of creosote, thus making the spear into two pieces. The shorter foreshaft, or dart, could penetrate its target, fall off from the spear, and be retrieved for use another time. If retrieval was not possible, the hunter could use the spear again with another foreshaft. Tom's practice foreshaft was carved of bone; its chert point was dull and chipped and attached to the foreshaft with pine pitch and sinew wrap. At the other end of the spear, three large feathers that looked like they might have come from the ancestor of a turkey served as fletching to stabilize the spear's flight.

Kevin watched as Tom placed the long shaft of his spear on top of the atlatl and secured it with the hook. He held the atlatl with the spear on it horizontally at eye level and took a step in the direction of the target. He pushed off from his back leg using his arm and wrist to throw the spear forward, landing on his front leg as he followed through. The hunting tool flipped around, sending the spear onward. There was a murmur of approval from the men and boys as the spear hit a melon and shattered it into half a dozen pieces.

Tom turned around with a wide grin. Chukotka picked up a spear and chose a foreshaft from a small pile on the ground. He followed the same procedure as his cousin, but his spear fell short of its mark by a few feet. Beside them, with a different elder as his tutor, Slats took the next turn. Kevin noticed his chest and arm muscles were more developed than Tom's, and he wondered how this would affect his performance. Slats scowled down the length of the shaft, took a few steps forward, then executed his lunge from back foot to front and sent the spear skyward with such force it sailed high over the target. Although he did not hit a gourd, the length of the throw was impressive, almost twice the practice distance, and this earned him a buzz from the instructors and participants, too.

While a couple of other boys took turns, the elder who was helping Tom and Chukotka gave Kevin a shaft and dart and made signals to Kevin to assemble them. Biting his lip in concentration, Kevin followed the elder's instructions, wishing Davy was with him to translate, but whenever he got confused, a pantomime solved the muddle. Finally he had his spear ready, resting on top of the throwing device. The spear bobbed slowly up and down as Kevin sought to steady it. When he had gained more control, the elder turned him toward the targets.

Out of the corner of his eye, Kevin looked at the other boys. The throwing movement reminded him of a pitch in baseball or a serve in tennis, both sports he had played. He took his stance, which the elder adjusted, and raised the spear. At a nod of the elder's head, he sent the spear toward the heavens. Well, it was supposed to have gone upward, but it landed a few yards in front of him with a great deal of churned-up dust. He heard Slats snicker, but this only made him more determined to improve. Tom took another turn, followed by Chukotka, then Kevin again. By the end of six rounds, he was doing much better, making it almost halfway to the target on his last throw.

Everyone knew that Tom and Slats were rivals, and the elders and boys watched with great interest as they prepared for their first hunt. Tom hit the target almost every time with his meditative, controlled aim, but Slats had the advantage of throwing strength. He also had a showmanship attitude about it that made the elder instructing Tom frown. At one point he said something to Slats, who responded with a snarl like a provoked dog. Kevin could make out only a few of the elder's words, but they had to do with Slats wasting his energy on bravado when it should be harnessed to achieve a successful kill, which would be of more use to the community than entertainment. A few rounds later the practice spears were all gone, and the boys sprinted out to retrieve them. Tom signaled for Kevin to come, too, telling him he was doing very well for his first time throwing a spear.

Kevin felt a burst of comradeship with the Clovis boys. He tore off his shirt (all the boys were bare-chested) and sprinted alongside them, happy under the blue dome of the day. A warm breeze ruffled his hair because he had also thrown off his cap. No one else was wearing a hat and he badly wanted to be included. He did not think he would go so far as to wear a loincloth—they did tend to expose things when you were running.

The boys roamed across the practice area seeking their spears, which had flown in all directions. Often they had skittered under tall grasses or popped over a rock, falling before or behind their targets. Tom retrieved most of his spears from the gourds and melons and grudgingly had to acknowledge that Slats had hit a few, too. The first target Tom had hit lay open with delicious-looking red flesh spilling out of it, reminding Kevin of a watermelon. Tom bent over to get him a slice. At that moment, Kevin saw a spear gyrating through the air toward them.

"Watch out!" he called, leaping forward and pushing Tom to the side.

As they tumbled away, the spear point entered the ground exactly where Tom had been standing a few seconds before.

"You saved my life," he said with great feeling.

Kevin opened his mouth to say something, he was not sure what, but the moment seemed to require it. All he could think of was, "You're welcome."

As they got to their feet, Tom reached for the spear. A boy ran up and said in a terrified voice, "That's my hunting spear, but I didn't throw it!"

The elders rushed to join them. No one had seen the incident; however, the spear did belong to poor Zhan, and because of this they assumed he was guilty. One of them grabbed the boy's hair and jerked him back, muttering fearsomely. Slats strolled up.

"What's the matter?" he asked.

"This one tried to kill To'meh!" an elder said, pointing at Zahn, who was weeping.

Kevin did not think so. He had watched the boys at practice, and he didn't think Zahn's aim was good enough to do what he was accused of doing. He had seen him miss his target almost every time, and if not for Kevin being there, Zahn would have been the worst of the bunch at spear practice. Slats had greater prowess than did the shorter, skinny boy who stood accused, and he also had the motive to remove Tom from the competition. Kevin thought the elders were aware of this, too, but they were at a loss how to explain the boy's spear that lay at their feet, its projectile point shattered, so it must have been thrown with some force. The men circled the boy, talking to each other. Tom told Kevin the boy's punishment could be severe. He added the elders would keep Zhan in isolation and a council would be formed to decide if he was guilty or not of wrongdoing. All of this on the eve of the mammoth hunt was unsettling because it would detract from the teamwork required to take down the giant beast.

Suddenly a boy pointed over their heads and cried, "The spirits are calling us. See, a mammoth!"

They all peered upward. Kevin thought the clouds looked like the frothy peaks of whipped cream on an ice cream sundae and not anything remotely like a mammoth—until suddenly, they did. A strong breeze from the upper atmosphere swooped down with massive fingers and sculpted the scattered cumulus into a towering shape resembling an elephantine head. Twisty tendrils of clouds provided two tusk-like shapes. The sun shining behind it created a halo of shooting golden lines resembling the crowns of saints in medieval paintings. Kevin was as awestruck as the others.

The men and boys became a little fearful and a muttered debate broke out about whether this heavenly sign favored the hunters or the intended hunted. They ducked their heads as they left the practice field, and some of them hunched their shoulders as if expecting a lightning bolt to come out of the sky. The cloud had cast a giant shadow over the plains, making the air cooler. Kevin was glad to put on his shirt and cap again. By the time they reached the camp, the celestial artist who had created the mammoth image had torn it apart and the sun shone unobstructed once more. The story of Tom and the near miss circulated quickly among the folk, but no one at camp commented on the mammoth head in the sky. Kevin thought this might be because none of them had been thinking about mammoths, and no one had seen anything but a big cloud momentarily blocking the sun. Mrs. Bowersock said that if you stared at clouds long enough you would see what you wanted to see, and Kevin decided that was what had just happened.

He watched as Zahn was led to the outskirts of camp where he was tied to a tree. His mother ran to him with cries of lamentation, bringing a gourd full of water and a slice of dried meat. He felt very sorry for the boy because he could still not shake the feeling that it had been someone else who had thrown the spear. He had not seen Slats on the practice field collecting spears until he had come up to them, and where was Rescalispel all this time? It was awful to think the son or father would want to harm Tom.

Kevin found Davy outside his aunt's house. He

was preparing to knap a large rock she had brought for him. He placed the rock on a leather hide over his knee and struck it with a round, fat hammerstone. A large flake slid away, exposing red jasper.

"I will make a spear point out of this for you," Davy said. He explained that once the jasper was out of the rock, he would use a tool he called a billet, made from the base of a deer antler, to chip smaller flakes. Finally, he would take the small, pointy part of an antler called a tine to push out even more delicate flakes to complete the point and make it sharp as a surgeon's scalpel. Kevin was impressed. He did not know how such a beautiful object as a projectile point could come out of a rock he would have stumbled over on a hike.

"Where are Savannah and Melody?" Kevin asked, realizing he had not seen them for a while.

"Away," Davy said vaguely, focusing on his work.

Kevin looked around, thinking they might have left him, but he saw Sombra still tethered to the tree and a circle of people studying her as she nibbled grass. He had a vague worry they might want to slaughter her, but there seemed to be an adequate supply of food at the camp after the bison kill, and the mammoth hunt was coming up, so he did not think this was going to happen. Then he saw a train of women and children including Irtyshi, Berul, Melody and Savannah coming toward the camp. Each had armfuls of flowers and branches, and one woman carried a skin filled with something that appeared to weigh a lot. Mitzi ran up to him and flopped down, panting. As they passed by Melody mouthed, "We need to go soon."

One of the girls glanced at him under her eyelashes, and he realized she was one of the brothers' cousins. When she saw him looking back she lowered her head modestly and smiled. Girls rarely paid attention to him in school, in spite of his ability as an artist. They seemed to prefer boys who were good in sports, or those from the next two grades up. Her attention gave him an unusual sense of pride in himself. He returned her smile.

"I wouldn't do that," Melody said, having excused herself from the women.

"Why?"

"I overheard a plot to marry you off to her."

"Really?" Kevin said, flattered.

"And Tom wants to marry *you*!" Davy said to Melody, without stopping what he was doing. More of the jasper inside the rock was showing, but it was a long way from looking like a projectile point.

"I'm sorry, I can't. I already have a boyfriend."

"You do?" Kevin asked.

"Yes. Well, I did until two weeks ago," Melody confessed miserably. "He told me he likes someone else now."

Kevin could not imagine anyone not wanting Melody for a girlfriend. He had a strong desire to punch the guy for hurting her feelings, whoever he was.

"And anyway," she said to Davy, "I'm much too young to get married."

"No, you're not. "My mother gave birth to To'meh when she was sixteen summers."

"Well, you see! I'm not that old yet. I'm still working toward my learner's permit." She added, "I'm going to get Savannah. They think she's someone special. They're always touching her hair."

As she walked away Davy asked, "What's a —what's a—"

"It's a piece of paper you earn so you can practice driving a car."

Davy looked at Kevin sorrowfully and said, "Oh Ke'on Eyer-eesh, I wish I could visit your world."

Kevin had thought about this also, but how could he explain to his parents where Davy came from?

"I wish you could visit my world, too," he said.

Davy nodded, and then he bent over the rock on his lap making as if to strike it.

"There is much discussion about our tribe and who should lead it," he said in a low voice so that no one else should hear. "It is rumored that our clan will join my aunt's clan after the mammoth hunt. Rescalispel has not been a good leader. The elders already prefer To'meh to Slats, and that does not go over well with Rescalispel. We try to resolve our issues together, but if there is ever a disagreement, our headman must stand for one side or the other. Rescalispel prefers using gifts to seal the matter, not wisdom.

"Whatever happens, our mother and little sister will leave with our aunt. Rescalispel wanted to marry our mother, but she did not wish to marry him. Because of this, Rescalispel forbade any elder to ask for her as wife. Without a provider and protector, she and my sister may die."

"But she has you and Tom to look out for her!"

"Someday we will have wives and children. We may marry someone from another tribe and leave her. One of us may undertake a great journey, as our clansman did who recognized the cry of the bird who lives near the sea. He was gone eight seasons and no one expected him to return, but he did. I would like to see the great waters. I would like to carve shells, too. Did you see the necklaces Irtyshi wears? The shells are from a place too far for a woman to walk with babies and children, or an old woman either.

"Irtyshi has found a husband for my mother," Davy added. He seemed to have forgotten the rock on his lap with the jasper inside. "He is from the clan my aunt married into."

"Will you and Tom go with her?"

"This I do not know."

Melody and Savannah, carrying the pink backpack, emerged from Irtyshi's house and were quickly surrounded by the women and children of the camp.

Some of the girls near Savannah's age held dolls that Kevin recognized. The little Clovis girls clutched them as if they were more precious than rubies. Savannah called out "Goodbye!" She smiled and waved as if she were a Disney princess. He heard promises going back and forth that she would return for the mammoth hunt, bringing her light from Soldorador to shine on the tribe's good fortune.

The brothers accompanied them to Sombra. Davy held the horse, stroking her nose. He spoke into her ear and she blew soft gusts from her nose back at him, content to enjoy his attention. Tom prepared to give each of them a leg up. When it was Melody's turn Kevin saw her smile at him.

As they rode away he asked, "Did you tell him the bad news?"

"You know as well as I do I won't be marrying Tom," Melody said, "but if it makes him feel strong and brave to think I might, I'll go along with it. This mammoth hunt is a big deal and dangerous, too. The mammoths don't line up like hairy melons in a row. I heard stories today about hunters getting trampled and eyes gouged out and stomachs sliced open."

Savannah had fallen asleep, and they agreed this was a good thing as they rode past the boy tied to a tree. Zahn gave Kevin a pleading look out of his large brown eyes. Kevin thought of the spear aimed at Tom today. He could not get out of his mind that it might have been thrown by Slats or Rescalispel.

When they were a little way from camp, Kevin looked back. The small settlement had disappeared around a bend. It was almost as if it had never been there at all and this was a dream. He had powerful dreams sometimes, but Melody's back was warm and the loose hairs in her braid tickled his cheek, and he did not think he would be aware of these sensations if he were dreaming.

"Where did you go with the women?" he asked.

"We walked around picking flowers and herbs to make garlands and wreaths for the ceremonies for the mammoth hunt. We also collected red dirt, which I think is called ochre, that the hunters paint their bodies with."

They were turning toward the arroyo when Sombra began to snort and dance. She pricked her ears in the direction of the waterhole where the bison kill had happened. Melody soothed the horse, clutching Savannah, who woke up.

"Kevin!" she said. "Look!"

A herd of mammoths was at the waterhole. Although they peered back at them inquisitively, the small group of bulls, cows and calves did not charge or run away.

"Gosh, they're big!" Melody said. "Shouldn't we ride back and tell Tom they're here?"

"I'm sure the tribe knows. After all, we saw them the other day on their way here, didn't we?" Kevin had the urge to pinch Melody for doubting him earlier, but he resisted. "Tom says they'll stay around the waterhole for a couple of days. They like the shade under the trees and scratch their backs on the trunks. They eat the plants until the area is almost bare. That's why they move on and why the Clovis people follow them."

"I'm hungry," Savannah said, patting the back-pack containing their lunch, which they had forgotten to eat. She appeared not at all fazed by the sight of the giant creatures. After her experience with the camelops, she seemed to have accepted Ice Age mammals as being bigger than what she was used to. And as Kevin considered this, he supposed dinosaurs were bigger than mammoths, so why be impressed?

They entered the arroyo and followed the line of the black mat until they emerged into the modern world, surprising a few people who had come to view the Murray Springs Clovis Site.

What stories we could tell them! Kevin thought as they rode away.

SIXTEEN
GOOD NEWS

WHEN THEY REACHED Spear Point Ranch, Melody put Sombra in the barn and Savannah chased chickens. Kevin went through the back door into the kitchen.

"Home so soon?" Mrs. Mason called from the hallway where she was watering houseplants. "I thought you would be gone a long time because you packed a lunch. It's not even noon yet."

Kevin looked at the clock on the stove. They had been away only a couple of hours, while he felt they had been in the Paleo-Indian world for most of the day. The morning seemed to have started out at a parallel time, but obviously it had not stayed that way. Time had sped up there as if the Earth twirled faster on its axis thirteen millennia ago. Melody came into the kitchen looking a little confused, too. Savannah followed her.

"What did you see on your ride?" Mrs. Mason asked setting the watering can beside the sink.

"Pinky-swear," Kevin whispered furiously to his sister.

"I didn't see any dinosaurs," Savannah said, although she looked ready to burst with her desire to tell Melody's mother what she really had seen.

"Goodness, look at your hands," Mrs. Mason said to Kevin. "Have you been playing in the dirt? And there are leaves all over your shirt, and it's torn, too."

Kevin thought this must have happened when he ripped it off to run with the Clovis boys, and his hands were filthy from scrabbling in the underbrush to retrieve spears that had not hit their targets. Guiltily, he realized he had paid more attention to spear practice than to figuring out how to get the obsidian point back in the case. Melody got a wild look on her face, and Kevin thought she must have forgotten about it, too, during the excitement of visiting the Clovis camp and seeing the mammoths on the way home.

The telephone rang and Mrs. Mason went to answer it. A huge smile stretched across her face when she returned to the children.

"Your mother is on her way to pick you up. She's got some good news for you."

"Daddy's coming home!" Savannah cried, jumping up and down.

Kevin felt like jumping up and down, too, but he

decided boys his age did not do this. He belted out a chesty "Hooah!" instead that ended in a squeak. His voice was going to change soon, Mrs. Bowersock told him. He made a motion to go through the kitchen and down the hall to the front door, but Mrs. Mason put a hand on his shoulder.

"Out the back, young man! My living room is clean and you are tracking God-knows-what on the bottoms of your feet."

Kevin turned obediently and went out the back door, Melody and Savannah following him. They ran around the side of the house to the front, where they found Mr. Mason standing by his truck. He was holding a bundle wrapped in a blanket and was about to place it in a big burlap sack.

"What is it, Dad?"

"It's the biggest seagull I've ever seen," Mr. Mason said. His arms were wrapped around a bird the size of Savannah. "Your mother heard on the radio that some seabirds were blown off course by a hurricane in the Gulf of California and carried all the way here from Mexico. This is one of them."

He parted the blanket to show the bird's head. Its eyes were as dark and shiny as volcanic glass, and its beak was massive and had sharp, tooth-like projections on both the upper and lower bills. A band of white spread across its eyes, and rings of orange and black lay around its neck, but the rest of the bird's feathers were an unappealing gray. Inside the blanket it beat its large wings in protest of its captivity. Suddenly it let out such a loud cry they jumped in surprise, and Mr. Mason almost dropped it.

"That bird sounds just like my tam-tam," Savannah said. "The one we heard today when we were with Tom and Davy."

"Who are Tom and Davy?" Mr. Mason asked.

Savannah shot a panicked look at Kevin and Melody, who looked helplessly back at her, unable to come up with a reasonable fib on the spur of the moment.

"They're my dinosaur friends," Savanah said finally, not meeting Mr. Mason's eyes.

Savannah was not a very good liar, either, Kevin thought, and if their mother did not arrive soon she might give something away. Come to think of it, if Savannah had answered they had been in a prehistoric camp with Clovis people she would have received the same reaction from Mr. Mason, which was to nod his head as if this made perfect sense.

"Can we keep it?" Melody asked. "We've got plenty of chicken feed."

"No, we can't. Seabirds don't eat grains like domestic fowl or drink fresh water; they're used to fish and saltwater. The radio announcer said anyone who finds a bird like this should bring it to a local wildlife center for a special diet and treatment of any injuries. If this guy or gal survives, it'll be rehabilitated and returned to the beach."

Kevin thought this bird did not look like any seabird he had seen in Hawaii. Savannah might be right when she said this was her totem that the Clovis man who had been to the coast had identified from its cry. It was a prehistoric seagull. It had straddled two worlds just as he, Tom, Melody and his sister had done, along with Mitzi and Sombra.

Mr. Mason began to stuff the bundled bird into the burlap bag, but it gave a great shove and kicked one of its webbed feet out from between a fold in the blanket, which flipped up. To Kevin's dismay, he saw the logo "Ace Tile and Grout." It looked like the same heavily padded blanket that had covered the projectile point display case in Melody's brother's bedroom. Mr. Mason succeeded just then in shoving the bird into the burlap bag and tying it up, after which he laid it gently in the bed of his truck. He opened the door and prepared to drive away.

"Dad," Melody said, laying a hand on her father's arm. "Where did you get that blanket?"

"It was handy. I found it behind the sofa after the workmen put the furniture back in the living room this morning. I'll return it to the tile company when I'm done with it, if that monstrous bird doesn't tear it to shreds first. In that case, I'll reimburse them for it."

"Oh my god," Melody said as her father drove away.

"If the workmen moved the display case back to

the living room," Kevin said, "your dad hasn't noticed the projectile point is missing."

"Hasn't noticed *yet*."

"What's your plan if he finds out?"

"*My* plan, Kevin Sinclair! How about *your* plan? You're the one who got us into all of this. We've got to get that spear point back tomorrow!"

"After the hunt."

"OK. After the hunt."

As Melody conceded this, Kevin thought she must have a soft spot for Tom, after all. Then he saw his mother's car pull off the road onto the driveway—and now he did jump for joy. He and Savannah, accompanied by Wyatt and Earp, barreled toward it. Mrs. Sinclair braked in a cloud of dust and leaped out to fold them in her arms.

The anticipation of his father's return to Fort Huachuca put the Clovis world out of Kevin's mind for the rest of the day until that evening when Mrs. Sinclair found an old white sheet and they fashioned a banner with "Welcome Home" and "We love you Dad" in big blue letters on it. Kevin had heard about artists attributing their creative skills to God or a divine power, and it was as if a spirit now guided his hand as he painted a mammoth with a spear embedded in its flank underneath the words.

"Your mammoth seems so lifelike," his mother commented. She added playfully, "Of course, I've never seen a real one."

Savannah drew a primitive sketch of Mitzi, recognizable only by her pink collar.

"I miss Mitzi," their mother said, and then bit her lip.

"She's OK," Savannah replied, matter-of-factly. Kevin held his breath, but Savannah did not miss a brushstroke, and to his relief his mother did not ask Savannah why this was so.

"When will Dad be home?"

"Oh, you know the military! Maybe tomorrow, maybe the day after tomorrow, or maybe next week. I hope they fly into Tucson sooner rather than later. We've got thunderstorms coming up this way from the hurricane off Mexico."

The same strong winds that blew in the seabird, Kevin thought. His mother sat down with a glass of wine to watch the news while he finished painting. When she got up for a second glass, she said, "Would you check on Savannah? I haven't seen her for a while."

He went down the hall to his sister's room. It was pink—pink walls, pink curtains, pink bedspread. It always made him a little nauseated to be in it. Savannah was sitting on the pink carpet with a dozen or more hair bows and fancy barrettes spread around her. She also had piles of headbands and elastics.

"Are you opening a salon?"

"These are for tomorrow. We're getting dressed

up for the mammoth hunt. I'm bringing hair things and Melody is bringing lipsticks and nail polish."

Kevin had not thought about something special to wear. He did not think a dress shirt and khaki pants like he wore to church would be appropriate, and his mother would be sure to ask why he was wearing them to the Mason's house. He would have to think about this overnight.

IN THE MORNING he woke up early, even earlier than on a school morning because he was so excited to get back to the Clovis camp. He smelled coffee and knew his mother was up already. Hungry, he ran to the kitchen in his pajamas. His mother looked a little tired. She said she could not sleep the night before thinking about all she had to do to get the house ready for his dad's return, on top of her job at the Fort.

"Savannah and I will clean our rooms before you take us to the ranch, and maybe Mrs. Mason can bring us back a little early so I can vacuum," he said. He thought the way time had worked out yesterday—when the Clovis world sped up and his present one did not—would be very convenient. Even as he thought this he knew there was no guarantee it would happen, but his mother's face brightened, making him feel warm inside because he had pleased her. As frustrating as she was sometimes, he loved her very much.

He ran down the hall and woke Savannah, who moaned and squealed when he threw off her covers and dragged her out of bed.

"Get dressed! Mom has to go to work today and I've promised we'd help her clean the house for when Dad gets home."

He did not really expect Savannah to be much help, but because she took so long to get ready to go anywhere, he had to give her a head start. When she went to the bathroom he began to tidy her room. Before she returned, he had made her bed and scraped everything off the top of her messy dresser into a drawer. He stuffed the hair ornaments into the backpack Melody had loaned her. He found Savannah's Halloween costume from the previous year in a heap on a chair. As he picked it up to throw it into the closet, she walked into the room and began to shriek.

"What's going on?" Mrs. Sinclair said, standing at the door. "Savannah, you'd think one of your dinosaurs just appeared in the window."

Savannah turned to look outside. She did not say anything and became very still, the way she did when she was not sure how to react in a new situation. Kevin looked out of the window, too. He knew enough about the clouds he saw in the distance to know that a big storm was approaching, although it was still a long way off. Here in Arizona you could see forever. But he didn't see any dinosaurs.

"Get dressed, Kevin, and hurry up, Savannah. I have breakfast on the table."

Kevin decided to wear a red and white checked long-sleeved shirt and clean jeans. To dress up the outfit a little he added a belt with hand-tooled decorations on the leather and a silver buckle with a turquoise stone in the center. It was not a very big buckle, but it was genuine silver, and he liked the turquoise with its blue and green colors and the fact the stone had come from a mine in a town nearby called Bisbee. Mrs. Bowersock had given it to him for his birthday. She said it had been her son's belt over twenty years ago. She had grandchildren now, but they were all girls and lived in Phoenix and weren't interested in a cowboy belt. Kevin wore it sometimes when she was over and he was not doing anything where he might get it dirty or scratched up, and this made her very happy.

After their mom had dropped them off at Spear Point Ranch, Mrs. Mason said, "My, you two look nice!"

Mr. Mason walked into the kitchen for a second cup of coffee. He looked over the steaming brim at them and his eyebrows went up.

"Kevin looks mighty fine and Savannah looks like —let me guess. Sleeping Beauty? Cinderella?"
"Snow White!"
Kevin had tried to persuade his sister to wear something more practical, but he had only succeeded

to the point of getting her to wear tights underneath the skirt so she would not chafe her legs while riding Sombra.

Melody walked into the room, and Mr. Mason's eyebrows practically met his hairline.

"And my daughter is Annie Oakley?"

Melody was wearing a tan leather riding skirt that reached to the tops of her boots, a vest to match the skirt, and an emerald green shirt with embellishments that sparkled as much as her eyes. She had tied a green ribbon around the crown of her hat, and, to hold it in place, a costume jewelry brooch.

Mrs. Mason said, "This is the outfit she wore when she was a rodeo princess."

"You were a real princess?" Savannah asked in awe.

"Yes," Melody acknowledged humbly.

Mrs. Mason handed out brown paper sacks. "Maybe you'll stay away long enough to eat lunch this time."

Mr. Mason asked, "Where are you going today?"

"To the Clovis camp," Savannah replied and then slapped her hand over her mouth.

Mr. Mason chuckled.

"The Murray Springs site is pretty informal," he said, "but as they say about baseball, 'You win some, you lose some, but you got to dress for all of them.'"

Melody just stared at her father.

"I think we should be going," Kevin said,

suddenly nervous. It was obvious Mr. Mason had not discovered that the obsidian projectile point was missing or he would have mentioned it, and Kevin was anxious to leave before he did. He still did not have a plan how to get it back. He hoped Melody had thought about it. He admired her for being able to pass the evening and this morning in a state of suspense, wondering if her father would notice.

"How did it go with the seagull?" Kevin asked to distract Mr. Mason as Mrs. Mason and Melody packed her saddlebags.

"It's like no seabird anyone has ever seen. Completely tore up the blanket and was working on the burlap by the time I got to the wildlife center. Almost bit the vet's finger off. It was going for blood, that's for sure!" He added, "The bird is expected to make a full recovery."

"I have to go to the bathroom," Savannah announced, swishing her yellow skirt and shifting back and forth on her flimsy, matching slippers. She tugged at her red cape and said to Melody, "Can you help me take this off? My mom tied it with a knot."

Kevin rolled his eyes.

"I'll help you," Mrs. Mason said, escorting Savannah out of the kitchen. Mr. Mason and Melody left for the barn. Kevin took the opportunity to run into the living room to look at the projectile point display case. The center position was empty, just as he thought it would be. He was heading back to the kitchen when he bumped into Mrs. Mason. He did not know how long she had been standing there.

"Missing something?"

Kevin almost fell over, terrified that she knew something was up.

"Uh, no. Uh, I have to use the bathroom, too." He raced down the hall and met Savannah halfway.

"Would you tie my cape back on?"

"No!" he practically shouted at her. "Go outside! Now!"

Mrs. Mason was feeding chickens when he hurried past her a few minutes later. She gave him an odd look. He decided he needed to appear nonchalant as if nothing unusual was going on and slowed to a saunter. He went over to the corral and began to rub Sid between the ears. Sid's dam walked over to them and tried to nibble his cap, reminding him of the camelops that had knocked Savannah's hat off. When Sombra came up, she laid back her ears and showed her big yellow teeth to the other mare.

"I think your mom suspects something," Kevin said as they left the ranch, finding the now-familiar cadence of Sombra's walk soothing to his frazzled nerves.

"I wouldn't doubt it. She's really good at seeing through bull—uh! I almost said a bad word. I must say you looked like the cat who ate the canary back there."

"What does that mean?"

"Ask Mrs. Bowersock. I learned it from her."

"You know Mrs. Bowersock?" he asked, touching the belt buckle.

"You think you and Savannah are the first kids she's ever babysat for? Brad and I had her for years."

The clouds he had seen out of Savannah's window that morning loomed ahead of them, bigger now and more formidable against an ever-darkening background. Mr. Mason had said the storm would take hours to reach them, and he'd added he had confidence in Melody to know when to return home. An erratic wind picked up Sombra's forelock and teased her tail. The horse appeared to like the weather, perhaps sensing the rain on its way, or maybe it was the increasing electricity in the air that tickled her nose. She pranced along the now-familiar trail to the arroyo, as if anticipating the more verdant valley with its abundant grasses ahead.

They came out of the draw to a sunny day, but in the distance Kevin saw the same storm clouds they had just seen thirteen thousand years forward, which he thought was worrisome because he didn't want the weather to cut short their adventure. He looked around to make sure they were really back in time, and indeed they were in the Pleistocene because the mammoths swayed around the waterhole the same as they had done the day before. He thought for a moment that it was a sad thing to kill such a magnificent creature, but in turn the mammoth gave sustenance to the hunters with its flesh; weapons, tools and bartering materials from its bones and ivory; and clothing and blankets from its hide. With such skill and risk required to obtain them, nothing was wasted. He wondered if today's target would be Big Eloise, whom Mr. Mason had mentioned when he had taken them to visit the Murray Springs site.

Their path led them into camp past the tree where the unfortunate boy had been tied. The rope swung empty, and Kevin thought of the Westerns he had seen where outlaws received their just desserts. Then they saw someone from camp running toward them. Sombra stopped, planting her hooves firmly to the ground, refusing to go forward.

At first they didn't recognize Davy. He had smeared the red, powdery earthen substance Melody called ochre across his face and neck. His eyes shone bright and owlish, and to complete the bird-like impression he had stuck short white feathers in his hair. Outlines of circles decorated his bare chest from his neck to his navel, likely painted on with charcoal from the hearths, and squiggly lines had been added on each side of these. He wore a loincloth that fell to his knees, more ceremonial than practical, and a necklace of several twisted strands of sinew on which had been strung a shell Kevin thought might be abalone; he had seen similar shiny rainbow-hued shells in Hawaii and recently in gift shops in Sierra Vista specializing in imports from Mexico.

Davy was obviously just as surprised to see Melody in her long, split riding skirt, Savannah in her colorful costume with its raised white collar resembling an Elizabethan ruff, and Kevin in his flashy checked shirt and jeans. But Davy stared hardest at Kevin's belt, where at this moment the silver buckle reflected the sun like a bursting star. Bronze had yet to be invented, and silver and gold were only shiny specks in rocks tumbling in fresh-water beds or buried underground. It must be a powerful image, Kevin thought, like the mammoth head in the clouds coming from the spirit world. Kevin did not want Davy to consider him otherworldly, even though he was, so he shifted slightly behind Melody into shadow. The sun fell on Sombra's gray rump instead.

The children dismounted. As they walked toward camp Kevin saw that a string of trees had been marked with a chalky substance that reminded him of Tom Sawyer's whitewash. The decorated trees made a sort of interpretive trail to the waterhole. In addition to geometric shapes, various animal forms had been painted on them, and also spears, a crescent moon and a sun. Davy explained that the drawings on his chest identified him as a member of his clan, and all the clans of his tribe were represented on the trees.

As they approached the camp, Kevin saw more men and boys bare-chested with identical or similar patterns. He expected to see the same markings as Davy's on Slats because the boys were related, as

Rescalispel was great-uncle to Tom and Davy. But Slats scowled at them as they walked past, wearing a different design of circles with dots in the center like bullseyes, and the wavy line appearing on one side only, the left side.

The women had also applied clan signs to themselves, often running the length of their bare arms and with the addition of circles of identical patterns around their necks.

"I didn't get the dress code memo," Melody said dryly.

Tom strode up wearing a smile as wide as the valley. His chest was painted like Davy's, but he did not have ochre on his face, and he explained today's initiates would be specially decorated for the hunt soon. The kids, he said, pointing to Davy, were dressed up as animals and birds to show they were related not only to each other, but also to nature. Tom's hair hung loose in thick, wavy locks, and he had tied a leather headband around his forehead. Kevin thought this gave him a strong resemblance to Native Americans. He remembered from a news article he had read on the Internet that American Indians carried DNA from their Clovis ancestors. Kevin's descendants from Europe had little, if any, Clovis DNA, and if some were detected, it was probably acquired after they emigrated to America.

Tom carried his spear with the obsidian point attached to a short dart at the end of it. Kevin was reminded they must not leave today without the projectile point. He knew Melody was thinking the same, and Tom followed their line of thought.

"I will give the spear point to you after the hunt so you may return it to your father," he said to Melody. "Our fathers share this gift from the earth, each in a different way: my father by its creation and your father by his appreciation of it. We are kin now. Welcome to my clan."

Davy said, "Ke'on Eyer-eesh, you are our brother, too, and S'anna our sister."

"Group hug!" Savannah called, but Tom would have none of it, resisting personal contact in the Clovis custom, and no one wanted to reach out to Davy because it was obvious he had been too liberal with the ocher paste; small particles of it had drifted off his body and stained his loincloth.

Hearing Savannah's voice, Mitzi appeared. They laughed because on each side of her muzzle someone had painted two lines of red.

One of the elders motioned to Tom, who left to join the men and boys to prepare for the hunt.

The cousin who had a crush on Kevin arrived to take Melody and Savannah to the opposite side of the camp where the women had assembled under the ramada. The fingers of the teenage girls fluttered over each other, braiding hair and adding flowers they had picked the day before, all the while chattering excitedly. They tied lengths of seed and bone beads around their necks and highlighted their bodies with clan symbols. Melody disappeared for a moment, and when she came back into view she was wearing her vest without the shirt underneath. Kevin wondered first with great curiosity and then with hot discomfort why she had removed it, but then he decided she was trying to fit in, just as he had the day before during spear practice.

One of the women gestured for Melody to sit down and began to accentuate her eyes with a dark liquid from a shallow bowl. Another drew Tom's clan symbols on her arms. They twittered merrily and said things to her she obviously did not understand, but she smiled kindly at them and reciprocated by painting nails and passing around lipsticks, which she demonstrated how to apply. Everyone erupted into giggles, much to Melody's evident confusion, when one girl added a crown of what looked like rosemary sprigs on her head. Davy smiled and told Kevin that in the language of flowers it meant love and a wedding on the way. Savannah was the focus of the little girls, who were as restless as chicks and chirruped as she clipped barrettes and tied ribbons in their hair. Elderly women were present, too, with features shrunken and caving in on themselves, reminding Kevin of decaying Halloween pumpkins complete with missing teeth in toothy grins.

Davy was called away to run an errand for his mother. With the camp divided between the men and the women, only the Storyteller remained in the center. He was chewing a couple of green leaves that were turning his lips the same color. The pupils of his eyes were as big and dark as dirty pennies. Kevin sat down next to him. He wondered if the Storyteller was looking past him or through him.

"The girl with hair the color of the sun, what happens to her?"

Kevin threw out the question, not expecting the chronicler to understand, but he did.

"Ah! You want to know the end of the story when we're only arriving at the middle."

"It was foretold she would come?"

"And so she has. She is one of the Early Ones."

"No she's not!" Kevin cried, surprising himself with his passion. "She's my sister. I saw her five minutes after she was born. She didn't come from the sky or a mountain or cross the sea to bring you good luck, or whatever you call it. She's a little girl who's going to start first grade soon."

They heard a scream above their heads and everyone in the camp looked up to see Savannah's totem flying above them. The Storyteller cackled as if this confirmed his words. Kevin wondered if the seabird had escaped from the wildlife center where Mr. Mason had taken it. The sight of the prehistoric bird with its great gray wings made the Clovis people pause what they were doing. The amusement and frivolity that had consumed the camp faded, and everyone began to focus on getting down to business.

Kevin got up and dusted off his pants. They had lost their laundered freshness and the tail of his red-checked shirt had slipped out of his belt. The men and boys with spears approaching made him uneasy. Melody's words from yesterday's visit rang in his ears: "Kevin, what did you get us into?"

SEVENTEEN

THE MAMMOTH HUNT

As the hunters paraded through the camp, the women and children left the ramada and surrounded them. Irtyshi led them in high-pitched trills and loud, rhythmical vocalizations. They swayed from side to side or bounced on their feet, and someone had taken up a drum so all began to chant together. The noise became deafening, and Kevin wondered if it was enough to make the mammoths turn tail and run from the waterhole in the opposite direction.

An elder escorted each boy, of which there were six. Charcoal representations of mammoth tusks swirled across their cheeks, foreheads and chins, distorting their features and making them almost unrecognizable. Davy scooted up to Kevin and told him the renderings fooled the mammoths into thinking the hunters were one of them, so they could get close. Kevin squinted at Davy to see if he really believed this to be true, and he did.

Among the boys, Kevin saw Chukotka and then, to his surprise, he saw the boy who had been tied to the tree. Zhan was walking freely with someone Kevin supposed was his father by the resemblance; he looked as skinny and meek as his son. Kevin turned to Davy for an explanation.

"The elders could not decide on a punishment. Indeed, they were not sure one should be given. The spear belonged to Zhan, but the aim was not his. It was far too accurate, the thrust of an experienced hunter, not a boy. I really don't know why Zhan is included," Davy added grumpily. "He has the all the spear-throwing ability of a flayer of hides."

Kevin knew Davy was again expressing his disappointment at not being among the hunters today, nor probably would he ever be considering his skill as a knapper.

"At first Rescalispel was all for punishment because he finds pleasure in blood," Davy continued, "but in the end he sided with the rest of the elders who had agreed that Zhan was innocent. They could not prove he threw the spear and decided it must be a god playing pranks."

"Do gods play tricks?"

"Of course! They like a joke, the same as we do. The elders decided that Zhan's parents must be out of favor with this particular god, and a price should be paid to appease the god to restore good fellowship to the hunt. Zhan's father has a knife made of ivory that Rescalispel covets, and as headman he demanded it in order to release Zhan. My aunt spoke up and said it was too great a settlement. She reduced the payment to two gourds and a fishhook. Rescalispel was not very happy, but he accepted the judgement."

"And if he hadn't?"

"Our great-uncle would have been sent out of the tribe," Davy said.

Thinking about it, Kevin decided it would be very dangerous to be on one's own during this epoch, given the primitive way of living, not to mention Ice Age carnivores. As he had often heard, there was safety in numbers with fellowship in the clan, and in knowing that your kinsmen would watch your back in the very literal sense of the phrase. To be cast out would result in certain death.

The chanting women and other members of Davy's tribe and Irtyshi's clan surrounded the novice hunters and elders and moved off toward the water-hole. Their voices subsided to whispers as they reached the first decorated tree, and there they settled as the hunters moved forward. Davy's mother took Savannah's hand. Kevin was relieved because his sister was liable to be swallowed up in the crowd in spite of her colorful costume. Melody mounted Sombra, the better to watch the hunters from a distance. Only the old men and women and the Storyteller stayed at the camp. The Storyteller was staggering about as if drunk.

As Kevin and Davy walked at the rear of the hunting party, Davy said in a low voice, "After the hunt the clans will split into two tribes, one under Rescalispel, and the other to leave with my aunt, as my mother and sister are doing. After Rescalispel laid eyes on your sister, he convinced some of the elders his leadership was confirmed by the fulfillment of the foretelling. While Rescalispel is not much favored as headman, others do not like taking orders from my aunt, a woman."

"We have many women leaders where I come from," Kevin said, although he could not think of one by name in the exciting moments before the hunt.

An elder spied them and gestured for them to return to the tribe; they could not be responsible for the safety of Tom's younger brother and his friend during a mammoth hunt. Davy grabbed Kevin's arm and indicated a slight rise in the land from where they could get a view of the waterhole. The boys crept under some bushes to conceal themselves, with Davy adding they would be beaten if they were discovered to have disobeyed orders. Kevin was both alarmed and thrilled by this; he had never been in such a dangerous position before with such an unpleasant penalty. Some of the white feathers on Davy's head had stuck to the shrub's twiggy branches, and the ochre on his face was running with perspiration. Kevin wanted to giggle at how silly his friend looked, but that would give them away, so he restrained himself with great difficulty, which caused him to fart. This resulted in both boys clasping their hands over their mouths to keep from whooping out loud. When they were able to control themselves, they saw the hunting party had halted and were crouched to the ground.

One of the elders blew on his fingers and waved them around in a gesture like a magician conjuring over his hat.

"Who is that and what is he doing?" Kevin whispered.

"He is our shaman, and he is blessing the hunt."

Suddenly something that looked like dice from a gambling table in Las Vegas flew up in the air.

"The stones fall where the gods send them, and this tells the hunters where to place themselves to attack."

Again, Davy spoke from the conviction of magical thinking, but Kevin was getting used to it and even finding it normal. It was a way of keeping in harmony with the natural world before scientific laws were discovered to explain things. The tribe had its own rules, like a religion, but Davy never called it that.

"The next toss will tell which hunter will cast the first spear."

Following the second throw, Tom stood up, frowning.

"I don't think your brother was chosen for the first shot," Kevin said.

Tom was speaking angrily to an elder, but the boys could not hear what he said. Rescalispel reached for the stones with a sly expression on his face, and Slats wore a triumphant smile. The elder said something to Tom, his expression indicating Tom must abide by his words. Tom nodded and hunkered down again, and the plan for the ambush continued for a few minutes until all the men and boys stood up. A sound like the ripple of the wind passed over the crowd half a football field length behind them.

The small band walked toward the waterhole and divided into two arms circling around to meet on the opposite side. A flock of birds startled by the Clovis hunters rose up out of the trees, agitating the mammoths, which made soft moans of unease. A large mammoth, the matriarch and leader of the herd, pealed out a sharp call. Kevin wondered if she was Big Eloise, but the hunters appeared focused on another female, slightly smaller and younger. By her side was a calf, cute as most baby animals are at whatever time in history, and when Kevin realized the dire consequences to this calf, he felt heartsick.

Another mammoth stood in the mud on the rim of the waterhole, which was not very deep to begin with. He tossed his huge head and took great draws of air into his trunk, but the hunters were still downwind and their presence not yet detectable. Kevin was impressed by the bull's tusks, which curved up and over his trunk; they were so long and heavy he wondered how the animal kept from pitching forward on its head. The mammoths began to shift anxiously away from the waterhole. The cows nosed their calves behind them, and some whose calves looked only a few months old nuzzled them under their bellies.

The matriarch's proboscis waved up and down like a conductor's baton, a signal that danger was approaching and they should flee. The bull tried to climb the slight incline from the waterhole to join the herd, but his great muscular hind legs had sunk so deep in the mud they refused to move. He scrabbled with his front legs, but they had no effect on pulling him out. The herd of fifteen mammoths seemed undecided what to do. They appeared reluctant to leave the bull, a valued member and, in times of danger, a good defense against predators.

The Clovis hunters drew closer, moving out of the denser vegetation onto the swath of grasses and low flowering plants surrounding the waterhole. The eyes of the matriarch grew wide as a man's fists, and she stamped her front feet. Kevin and Davy could feel the ground shake from where they were concealed. The bull was exposed and vulnerable, and he twisted violently, only to sink further into the soft mud. He grunted in terror from what would surely be his deathbed from the hunters, or, if left to live, from the agony of starvation if he stayed stuck. It seemed the latter would happen as the hunters moved past him toward the herd seeking tenderer prey.

The mammoths had now backed away from the waterhole onto slightly more elevated, dryer ground, still apparently undecided about leaving one of their own. They seemed not to have any experience with human predators. The humans were small creatures—you could stack three of them, one on top of the other, just to reach the biggest mammoth's shoulder—and the tallest elder would have had to stand on tiptoe to pat the head of a yearling.

Slats led the boys, and the experienced hunters following them, pace by pace. Slats' spear rested on his atlatl. The other initiates had readied their weapons, too, and followed him until they were within throwing range of the massive beasts. The mammoths huddled together, their young in the center, becoming a great wheel of swaying gray bulk with menacing tusks.

An elder of the tribe called out and pointed to the young female mammoth. She and her calf had moved a few feet to the right. The terrified calf ran in circles around his mother. The frenzied cow scolded him, angling her body this way and that to coax him back to the safety of the herd. At one point she pivoted to the front, exposing her chest and neck as she tossed her head toward the calf. Slats raised his spear and fell back on one foot in preparation to throw. He sent his spear straight and true at the female mammoth, where it lodged in her breast at the juncture of neck and shoulder. Now the other boys aimed and threw their spears, too, a deadly rain of shaft and dart points. The elders followed with a cascade of their own. The cow stood stunned by the pain. Another elder took this moment to run forward with a thrusting spear with a bone foreshaft, its blade almost two feet long, and plunge it into her heart. Blood spurted in a cataract of red as the mammoth's heart pumped its last beats. She took a step toward her calf. Her legs buckled underneath her and she dropped to the ground. Again, Kevin felt the earth tremble.

The hunters cheered. The mammoths shifted back and forth, trying to make sense of the unexpected death of the cow, but they did not make any move to leave. The calf stood by his mother, dumbfounded. His small proboscis, like a child's hand, reached out to stroke her body, and Kevin could hear his little bleats of distress. Slats, Tom, Chukotka and the other three boys ran up to the fallen mammoth. They began to pull out their spears, examining the points to see if they were chipped or whole. Tom had removed his spear, too, and pulled off the dart with the obsidian spear point. He waved it aloft. To Kevin's eye where he still crouched next to Davy, it looked unblemished. Then Tom stuffed it into a leather pouch and affixed another dart point to his spear. Immediately following, a great bugle—recognizable as a call to battle—echoed around the waterhole.

Like everyone else, including the seasoned elders, Kevin had assumed the bull elephant was stuck in the mud for good. No one had paid attention to it. But now, to everyone's horror, they watched as it pulled itself free of the mire with a great sucking sound and heaved its body forward. The matriarch trumpeted encouragement. The small ears at the sides of the mammoths' domed foreheads swiveled around as their attention focused on the bull.

Slats' spear had penetrated deep into the dead cow's neck, a fine first shot, but also making it difficult to retrieve the dart point. He was distracted as he struggled to pull it out, and although he must have heard the bull's cry, it was obvious he did not interpret it as the warning of imminent attack. When he looked up, the bull was almost upon him. Then a spear whistled past his ear and entered the eye of the bull, causing the mammoth to skid to a halt. The giant began a dance of agony. A few more spears flew toward it and missed because they were thrown in haste. No one had expected the attack, and few were prepared to throw again. An elder called out in pain as one of the boy-hunter's spears lodged in his thigh. Another dragged him behind the fallen cow where the rest of the hunters had taken cover, fumbling to re-arm themselves. Suddenly the bull took off, running toward the south. The spear shaft broke away, but the dart point remained in its eye. He was soon lost to view on the grassy horizon.

Tom went forward to retrieve his shaft with its fletching of feathers, for it had been his spear that had half-blinded the mammoth. The hunters swarmed around him, calling out congratulations. The waiting crowd behind them celebrated with cheers, ululations, and yips accompanied by rattles made from dried gourds fashioned like castanets. Any remaining wildlife in the trees and understory surrounding them rose on wings or scurried away. And so did the calf.

Kevin and Davy emerged from under the bushes and joined the throng. Some of the tribespeople carried butchering tools because the dead cow was too big to transport back to camp in one piece. Men and women surrounded the mammoth and argued about where to place the first cut. Others picked through the grasses for projectile points, retrieving those that were usable again as spear points or, if broken, could be knapped down to knives and scrapers. The points that had shattered into unworkable pieces were left where they lay.

Tom, Slats, and the other initiate hunters and their escort elders were having a small ceremony. Kevin saw one of the elders place a thumbprint of blood from the cow on each boy's forehead. The boys looked solemn, but as soon as the elders had finished and walked away, they grinned at each other. Kevin noticed a couple of them were shaking, as if the stress of the hunt had finally caught up with them. Zhan turned away with tears in his eyes. He had acquitted himself well, but it had been a strain on him, more so than most. Girls came up shyly to offer water; soon these hunters—boys this morning, young men this afternoon—would be seeking wives. Little children reached out to touch them as if the gods themselves had appeared on earth.

Kevin and Davy ran to Tom and danced around him. Not far away Slats stood alone, his father having gone to help some of the men who had decided to begin the slaughter by cutting through the mammoth's thigh to separate the leg from the body. Tom excused himself from the boys and walked up to Slats.

"Good first throw, cousin. You brought her down quickly."

Slats looked confused, not used to compliments. It was as if no one had ever taught him how to respond to one. Certainly, Rescalispel had not.

"Where I come from," Kevin whispered to Davy, "we say *thank you*." He said this in English.

Slats heard him. He studied Kevin with his quick, sharp little eyes, and then turned to Tom and said very quietly, *"Thank you."* He lowered his broad brow and appeared deep in thought. Finally, he looked up and added, as if this were a great effort, "And *thank you* for saving my life." He started to walk away but came back. "It was I who threw Zahn's spear on the practice field."

Slats got a defiant look in his eyes, as if challenging them to respond, but no one did. Then his expression changed from the triumphant warrior of a few minutes ago to that of a boy who feels remorse, reminding Kevin that he really was a boy, only a few years older than he was, a boy doing a man's job for the first time today.

"What do you say when this happens in the land you come from?" he asked Kevin.

"*I'm sorry.*"

"*I'm sorry*," Slats said to Tom.

"You should say you're sorry to Zahn, too," Kevin added.

Slats' eyes flashed with their old insolence. "That will be the day," Kevin heard him mutter in the Clovis language as he left.

ALL THIS TIME the mammoth herd had remained close by, reluctant to leave the dead female, their fallen comrade.

Melody rode up. Tom brightened, clearly waiting for her to tell him how brave he had been, but she looked around the busy scene and asked, "Where did the baby mammoth go?"

"He ran away," Tom replied, annoyed.

"Will he come back?"

"I doubt it. He was frightened. He'll run until he can't run any farther, then he'll realize he's lost."

"What will happen then?"

"He'll probably get eaten by a cat, a lion or a bear," Davy piped up.

"You have bears here, too?"

"Yes," Kevin said. "I saw one on a Pleistocene website. It's called a short-faced bear and is much bigger than—"

"You can't let that baby die! He's just lost his mother!"

"We cannot do anything about it," Tom said.

"Well, I can do something about it! I'm going to bring him back."

With that, Melody swung Sombra in the direction the calf had taken and urged the horse forward. She charged through the working tribespeople, who parted to let her pass, and emerged onto the open plain. Soon the horse and rider were gone from view.

Savannah rushed up, her arms painted with the wiggly lines of Tom's clan.

"Where did Melody go? Oh, no!" she cried, seeing the dead female mammoth up close in a pool of blood with a white leg bone exposed and her fur and flesh ripped away from the ribcage.

Irtyshi and a small group of women approached, Tom and Davy's mother among them. Berul took the distraught child by the hand and walked back toward camp. Savannah sniffled a little, but soon she was skipping along, swishing her Snow White skirt and calling out the names of the Seven Dwarfs. Whenever she passed, people stopped what they were doing and smiled at her, still marveling at her bright blue eyes and her hair the color of sunflowers, an ancient plant going further back in time than the Ice Age, and many of which nodded pleasantly around the waterhole as the breeze picked up.

Irtyshi was praising the new hunters. Beyond her, Kevin saw Rescalispel standing by the carcass, watching Savannah depart. He thought Slats' father took too much interest in his little sister, and he vowed to keep a better eye on her, especially since Davy had told him Rescalispel was using her to confirm his leadership of the tribe.

Rescalispel turned back to butchering the mammoth. Kevin was sure now she was Big Eloise, the name the anthropologists at the Murray Springs Clovis Site had given the skeleton when it was first discovered. He watched as Rescalispel slashed at the carcass with abandon, slicing through precious tendons. One of the elders scolded him for not taking care; the strong fibrous tissue could be used for lashing blades to shafts or twisted into strong cordage. Serving as headman did not place Rescalispel above criticism in this small, primitive society where everyone watched everyone else continuously. Men and women were vocal about passing judgement, especially when it came to survival.

The mammoth herd grew restless. They raised their trunks and sniffed the air, heads turning in the direction Melody had gone. Something in their attitude caused people to pause, and a few of the men reached for their spears. The injured bull might be coming back, after all.

"There's the calf!" Kevin called out suddenly, "And I see Melody!"

The mammoth calf was bobbing slowly toward them, obviously fatigued, and Sombra followed, occasionally nosing the calf's flank to encourage it along. Melody rode straight in the saddle and made an impressive sight in her vest, skirt, boots, and hat, which she had slammed over the rosemary crown as she raced after the calf. She looked every inch the hero.

The calf caught sight of the herd and headed that way, but then the wind shifted and he picked up his mother's scent. Frantic, he quickened his pace and veered toward her. Melody kicked Sombra into action. The horse swerved around the calf and came to a stop directly in front of the dead mammoth, assuming the position to spring, her hindquarters up, her forelegs down. The calf made an advance toward its mother. Sombra pivoted sideways. The calf bolted in the other direction, but Sombra was again in front of him. Melody kept the reins gentle on Sombra's neck; the horse knew what to do. Then by an unseen movement, Melody asked Sombra to rustle the mammoth calf over to the herd, which watched in stunned amazement as the calf bore down on them,

Sombra on its tail like a hound to a fox. The matriarch figured out the intention first. She swung around on the herd behind her and charged through, opening a path for the calf to enter, which he did as fast as his short legs could carry him. Just as the herd closed ranks, Sombra slid to a halt inches away from the tusks of the defensive adults. Melody yelled, "Sombra, head for home!" Hearing this command, the horse spun on her rear hooves and raced back from where she had come, which was toward the tribe, who by now were cheering and jumping wildly up and down.

"Melody's a rodeo princess," Kevin said proudly, although no one could hear him in the uproar and nobody would know what a rodeo princess was.

The mammoth herd moved off, headed in the southerly direction in which the bull had gone, their short stubby tails beating time on their weary haunches.

EIGHTEEN

THE FEAST

"I SAW a ring around the moon last night," Davy said as they walked back to camp. He pointed to a haze streaming out at right angles behind the mountains, indicating the direction of the storm front. "And I heard a dire wolf howl. When that happens together, it means rain."

They had stayed behind at the butchering site to collect some of the projectile points. Davy showed Kevin hundreds of flint flakes that lay scattered where his people had sharpened their tools, for this and on previous hunting trips. As they passed the bull mammoth's huge footprints in the mud, Kevin marveled that they could be preserved for thousands of years.

When they reached the camp the festivities had already begun. Kevin saw Slats, Tom and Melody sitting in positions of honor next to Irtyshi under the ramada. Slats was there for throwing the first spear, enabling the other hunters to successfully take down the female. Tom sat next to him, praised for saving Slats' life. Melody was acclaimed for bringing the baby mammoth back to the herd. In practical terms, the Clovis people would not have gone after it, not being sentimental, but they admired her showmanship.

The new initiates had washed off their mammoth-hunting paint, leaving a ruddy glow on their brown cheeks; their eyes were bright and their attitude carefree now that the hunt was over. With their skinny necks and arms, they looked too young to have pursued the gigantic beasts, even though their chests and shoulders had begun to round out with burgeoning muscles. Soon they would become thick and slightly stooped like their elders, stronger than young *Bison latifrons*, bold as the lion *Panthera leo atrox,* and clever as the jaguar, whose descendants still roamed the mountain ranges between southern Arizona and Mexico. Melody had unbraided her hair, which lay loose around her shoulders. She looked very pretty, and more Clovis boys than just Tom were looking at her with interest.

Davy asked Chukotka why Tom had been unhappy about the second toss of the stones before the hunt, the one that determined who would throw the first spear. His cousin said Rescalispel had made the toss and that Tom thought he had calculated it to favor his son. Now this was in the past, the hunt had been fruitful, only one man had been injured and he was already bandaged and feasting, and the hunters had shown great bravery in the face of certain death from the panicked bull. And yet no one was attributing this to skill and initiative, but to the good fortune Savannah had brought them.

"S'anna! S'anna!" Kevin heard from time to time.

Savannah had her own place of honor next to Irtyshi. It did not take Kevin long to figure out it was a higher position than that of the two boys and Melody. Again he had a niggle of doubt that this was somehow not right and possibly dangerous, but he was not used to trusting his instincts. He thought perhaps they were like Davy's predictions: you could attribute them to spirits when you could not explain something logically.

Kevin realized he was hungry. He smelled meat cooking and following his nose, saw some of the women bending over hearth fires. They prodded large hot stones from the red embers and threw thin slices of meat on them to cook, producing the same sizzle as a steak when his dad tossed it on the barbecue. Baskets containing heaps of berries and other fruits were being passed around, along with a pudding-like mush in a large calabacita shell out of which people were taking swipes with their fingers to put in their mouths.

Savannah ate a few berries, and a short time

later lay her head in Irtyshi's lap and fell asleep. The lady looked surprised but gazed down at the little girl with a gentle expression, eternal for any mother in any millennium. When mammoth meat was offered to Melody she made a face such as someone might do when they see a cricket leg floating in their soup. Kevin heard her say "I'm a vegetarian," although he knew this was not true. He was determined to try a slice just to say he had eaten mammoth, and he found it tasty and a little chewy; it was also somewhat gamey like the javalina meat his father had brought home after a hunting trip shortly before he was sent to the Middle East. Mitzi darted among the seated tribespeople, who fed her treats. In fact, Kevin thought, she looked quite roly poly.

After the feast they gathered in the open air, cooler now from the gusts blowing under the clouds to the east. Kevin was glad for his long-sleeved shirt and Savannah, waking up, drew her red cape around her. Melody disappeared and returned wearing her green blouse. She had a dreamy expression on her face and sat a little closer to Tom than Kevin had seen before. Davy had picked up her hat while she was gone and was studying the decorative pin on the headband.

"What stone is this?" he asked.

"That's just plastic," Kevin said, but when Davy looked interested he added, "Modern man made it.

You won't find it in rocks or streambeds. I think obsidian is much nicer."

After he said this Kevin remembered the projectile point—obviously Melody had forgotten about it again, too—but before he could ask Tom for it, the six new hunters stood up.

"What's going on?" he asked.

"They are going to reenact the hunt!" Davy said.

Accompanied by drummers, the boys danced around each other in a pantomime beginning with the double toss of the stones, followed by sneaking around the waterhole toward the herd, and then the death throes of the cow and the charge of the bull. A low, singsong chant from both women and men accompanied the performance and crescendoed until a couple of the dancers acted out Melody's wild ride and the return of the calf, which ended the story to shouts and cheers. The Storyteller leaped into the middle of the boys and began to shout out Savannah's name in the Clovis language and a long string of words that sounded like babble. Many of the tribespeople jumped up to join them, mimicking the hunters or mammoths. Kevin thought they had gone a little crazy. He smelled something sour and sharp like alcohol and was surprised to see a milky substance passed around in gourds. Everyone but the smallest children was taking a swig. Davy started toward the nearest one, but Kevin pulled him back.

"It's time for us to leave, but we need the spear

point first. Find your brother and Melody. I'll get my sister. We'll meet by Sombra."

Kevin could not see Savannah in the moving mass of capering and laughing bodies. He pushed his way to the ramada, but she was not there, either. He thought she might still be with Irtyshi and easily located the boys' aunt, the tallest person present. He ran over to her and was relieved to see Savannah by her side.

"Ma'am," Kevin said, "We must go home now. Say good-bye, Savannah."

Savannah looked up at Irtyshi and crooked her finger to indicate the lady was to bend down. When she did, Savannah gave her a kiss on her cheek. Irtyshi put her hands on Savannah's shoulders and squeezed gently as her own expression of affection, after which she took the necklace with the beautiful pink shell on it from the several she wore and placed it over Savannah's head. Kevin heard Rescalispel's voice as he came up behind them, but was not sure what the man said because his words were slurred as he wiped away some of the pale liquid from his mouth. Irtyshi whirled on Rescalispel and addressed him in language Kevin did not understand, but her tone indicated she had lost patience with the head-man's attitude.

"Let's go!" Kevin said to Savannah, seeing this as a chance to get away without being noticed. He was afraid they were going to be caught between two warring clans.

"Where's Mitzi?" Savannah wailed, pulling against his hand as he dragged her along. Her flimsy yellow shoes shot up plumes of dust in resistance.

"We don't have time to find her!"

They heard a great roar from the crowd behind them, and Savannah gave up and ran with him to a tree at the outskirts of camp where Sombra was tethered. Davy, Melody and Tom were already there. Kevin could tell right away something was wrong.

"Look!" Melody said, holding out the projectile point on the palm of her hand. "It's chipped! Dad will be furious. We can't put it back like this. It's worse than having it go missing."

Tom seemed confused by what Melody was saying. Davy jumped in to translate and his brother said something quickly in response.

"To'meh says spear points break all the time. It is the nature of spear points."

Lightening flashed on the horizon. They looked at the sky and the dark clouds rolling over their heads; the setting sun peeked through in a desperate game of hide and seek. A cold gust of the advancing storm reached them and blew Sombra's tail across Melody's face as she stared in desperation at the projectile point.

"I can fix it," Davy said.

"Fix it? How?"

"I'll take my billet and reshape it. It only needs a little work to make it look like it was before."

"Hurry! We haven't much time."

Melody thrust the projectile point at Davy.

"Oh, I can't fix it now. My tools are at the camp."

Davy took the point, wrapped it carefully in a piece of leather, and placed it in his pouch.

Tom studied the shell Savannah was wearing. He said, "Irtyshi gave this necklace to you as a parting gift. The clans are dividing. Rescalispel will stay here with his kinsmen, and my aunt will rejoin her husband's relatives." He waved toward the east, and Kevin thought he might mean they were going to New Mexico. If they were traveling to the next state over it would be a long walk. It was highly likely Irtyshi was right; she would never see Savannah again. If Tom and Davy chose to go with her, the five of them would be parting, too.

Tom looked at Melody, and Davy looked at Kevin. For a moment, they let this news and its consequences sink in. Then Savannah squealed and jumped up and down, too terrified to speak. They all turned to see where she was pointing.

A dark mass, darker than the turbulent, storm-tossed sky, advanced toward them, composed of so many people that the camp was obscured behind it. One person broke free from the crowd and sprinted toward them. It was Slats. He was not carrying a spear, although most boys carried knives at all times. Tom reached for his.

"Creatures from another world!" Slats called out as he came up to them. "You must depart! My father comes to capture S'anna and keep her for his clan and later claim her as wife. I am telling you this because To'meh saved my life today. Now I save one for you."

"Rescalispel will have to fight me for her first!" Tom said.

"Our kinsmen are coming, too. You can't defeat them all, mighty hunter!" Slats gave Tom one of his ironic grins. Then he turned to Kevin. "Go!"

Melody, Kevin and Savannah mounted Sombra.

"What about the spear point?" Melody asked, turning the horse toward the arroyo.

"I'll send you a sign when it is ready," Davy shouted, the wind almost pushing the words back in his mouth.

As they galloped away Kevin looked over his shoulder. He saw the throng reach the boys. Two elders grabbed Slats, and a man he was sure was Rescalispel swung his fist and sent him to the ground, where he clutched his head. Tom and Davy were swallowed up. Then Sombra reached the bend in the path and the Clovis people were lost from view.

NINETEEN
CONSEQUENCES

As the three of them galloped away, they heard a dire wolf howl close by. Another answered. Rain began to sting their eyes and the wind pummeled their faces. Kevin remembered what one of his schoolmates had said about arroyos flooding and the inability to cross them until the water went down. He worried about getting home.

With the Clovis mob far behind them now, Melody slowed Sombra to a walk. Clouds shrouded the moon and stars in the Pleistocene world. In the darkness the mare picked her way carefully, just as Mr. Mason had said a good horse did on uneven, rock-strewn ground. With his hands around Melody's waist, Kevin could feel her body relax when Sombra entered the arroyo. The further they went into it, the less the rain fell, and then the rain was gone. The desert gorge was muddy as if it had seen its share of precipitation earlier, but its floor was nowhere near as grasping as the muck that had held the bull mammoth prisoner. Now the moon peeked through the clouds. To his amazement, Kevin realized they had been away an entire day.

Suddenly Sombra stopped. Melody urged the horse forward, but the mare shook her head so emphatically her bit rattled. Her ears swiveled in front of her and her nostrils flared. Kevin wondered if she detected dire wolves, but then he reasoned they were in the twenty-first century again where they didn't exist. Melody kicked Sombra. When she did not respond, she kicked harder. Finally the horse moved reluctantly along the wash, tossing her head the way the matriarchal mammoth had done at approaching danger. As they reached the bank with footholds wide enough for Sombra to climb up to the Murray Springs Clovis Site, they heard it: a great, roaring sound, like an ocean booming in the desert.

"Flood!" Melody cried, flapping the reins on each side of the reluctant horse to impel her forward. Sombra valiantly tried to mount the bank, but it was slick from the recent rainfall. She slid back down and tried again. Then she began to whinny and prance in a circle.

"Hold!" Melody called to the rodeo horse, who immediately froze in her position. "Kevin, you have to get off. See that hanging tree root? Use it to pull yourself up."

He let go of Melody and grabbed the root that was sticking out from the arroyo wall. He was on higher ground in a few seconds. Melody passed Savannah up to him. She tried again to get the horse up the bank, but Sombra slipped back as before. The roar of the water grew louder and time was running out.

"Melody, get up here! You have to let Sombra run for it!"

Melody paused, her face like stone. Then she vaulted off Sombra, and Kevin pulled her up next to him, wondering where he got the strength. The horse paced back and forth, looking up at Melody in desperation. The girl rose to her feet. She flung her arms out and, using the same command she had hollered at the horse to send her flying after rescuing the mammoth calf she yelled, "Sombra, head for home!"

Sombra turned and fled. She had only just disappeared around a turn in the bank when tumbling water with froth on top like surf rushed past them. The water bumped into the bank and surged left, following Sombra, careening half-way up the arroyo walls, only a couple of feet under the black mat. It seemed impossible that the water would not overtake the horse.

"We should have left earlier," Melody moaned. "No projectile point is worth my horse."

Savannah said, "I'm cold."

"Let's go," Kevin said, taking his sister by the hand. He patted Melody on the back with the other, thinking this was a feeble gesture at her great loss, but she nodded in thanks, looking as if she were as old as Mrs. Bowersock.

"I can't walk," Savannah said in despair, looking at her mud-encrusted feet. Kevin saw she was shivering and had lost her flimsy Snow White shoes.

"I'll carry you," Melody said, lifting the little girl in her arms.

The water continued to churn below them. After a few minutes pacing back and forth, they found the path to the highway. The clouds had rolled away. The moon had waxed to its first quarter and, pale and dim as it was, it glimmered enough off the path, still slick from the rain, to guide them. As he walked, Kevin looked up at the stars. There were so many he wondered why they did not bump into each other; the universe seemed a crowded place when viewed like this. His science teacher told them that light from the nearest star took four years to reach Earth. He felt as if that same number of years had passed since Mr. Mason had driven them to the Clovis site after Mitzi went missing, a caveman stood in his backyard, and a spear point disappeared.

When they reached the highway, they saw headlights coming toward them. Melody waved. The car turned out to be a county police vehicle.

"Well, Miss Melody, Mr. Kevin and Miss Savannah," the officer said. "Your parents are worried about you!"

"How did you know my name?" Savannah asked as she slid into the back seat.

"Tonight, everybody knows your name," he said. As he pulled onto the highway, he reached for his radio and activated the lights on the roof.

Kevin felt a little thrill as they zoomed down the highway because he had never ridden in a law enforcement vehicle before. When he turned to Melody to see if she was excited, too, he saw her frantically rubbing away tears from her cheeks. His pleasure in the ride faded. He stared at the bright lights on the dashboard in front of him. They made the darkness outside the windows appear as black as obsidian.

The bumpy stretch of the unpaved driveway brought them to the front of the Mason's house. All the lights were on and another patrol car was there, along with the Sinclair's car. Mr. and Mrs. Mason, their mother and a police officer were waiting for them outside. Wyatt and Earp trotted back and forth as a welcoming committee.

When all three children had been hugged, established to be unhurt, and the condition of their clothes exclaimed over, Mr. Mason asked as the patrol cars drove away, "Where is Sombra?"

"There was a flood in the arroyo, Dad. She couldn't climb the bank because it was too slick from the rain. I turned her loose."

"That's a twelve-thousand-dollar investment you

just let go, plus a good saddle," Mrs. Mason said. She had recovered from the emotional reunion very quickly. "What were you doing out so late and where exactly *were* you?"

"We were at the Clovis camp," Savannah said.

Neither Kevin nor Melody denied this. They hadn't had the energy to agree on an alternate story on the walk to the highway. In a way, Kevin thought, it was a relief to come clean, even though he knew they would not be believed. He wondered if the loony bin had beds for children.

"After the mammoth hunt we had a feast," Savannah continued, "Then it got dark and Irtyshi gave me this. See?"

The adults peered at the pink shell necklace Savannah wore.

"Where did you really get it, darling," their mother asked. Then she drew a weary hand across her forehead, appearing not to care, at least for the moment. "Savannah has a vivid imagination," she added. "You know, dinosaurs and such."

Mr. Mason seemed interested.

"Since you were at the Clovis camp, I wonder if you could tell me if you saw my missing projectile point there?"

"Oh, George," Mrs. Mason broke in. "Don't play into this game. The children need to change into dry clothes. Look at you, Melody. You've ruined your rodeo outfit and lost your hat, too."

"We should be going home," Mrs. Sinclair said, shuffling Kevin and Savannah to the car. Kevin watched as the Masons ushered Melody into the house. She did not turn around to wave good-bye.

When they arrived home, Mrs. Sinclair helped Savannah out of her costume and ran a bath for her.

"Where's Dad?" Kevin asked, having changed into his pajamas.

"He's in Washington, D.C., for a debriefing before coming home."

"What's a debriefing?"

"It's when you tell the story of what happened on a mission. Or on an adventure, as in your case."

His mother looked pointedly at Kevin when she said this.

Savannah called from the bathroom. Kevin took the opportunity to run to his room and jump into bed. He turned out the light. He hoped his mother would think he was asleep and not ask any more questions. But sometime later she came into his room and sat down next to him.

"Kevin, I'd like to hear the truth about where you spent the day, but I'll let your father handle this when he comes home. You are not to let the blame lie with Savannah's invisible friends, either. I must say, that shell is beautiful, although it looks very old, ancient even. I'm glad you're back safe and sound."

"Me too, Mom."

Early the next morning Kevin heard the phone

ring. By her tone of voice he could tell his mother was having a conversation with his father, although he could not hear what she was saying through his bedroom door. He fell back asleep. When he woke up an hour later he went to the kitchen, but he did not see his sister.

"She's still sleeping in my bed," his mother said, beginning to cook breakfast. "She kept calling out for Davy and Tom, whoever they are, and once she woke up shouting 'Rescue me pal,' or something like that. I had to cuddle her until she fell asleep again. One egg or two?"

"Two, please."

His mother seemed in a chatty mood. She told him his father would call again tonight, and she was going to get a raise at work, which made a trip to Disneyland closer than ever. Mrs. Bowersock had fully recovered and would be able to babysit again, so Melody would not be watching them any longer. School was starting on Monday. Then she said, "Do you remember the big bird Mr. Mason found, the one he thought was a seagull? Well, it's been confirmed it's a—here, he wrote it down for you."

Kevin read the slip of paper she handed him: *Osteodontornis orri*, or giant, bony-toothed prehistoric seabird. Miocene.

"What's a Miocene?" she asked. "You seem to know a lot these days."

"It's a period of time between the Jurassic and the Pleistocene."

"What does that mean?"

"Between the dinosaurs and the mammoths," Kevin said, getting a funny feeling in his stomach. Why was prehistory being tossed around like his juggling balls? Clovis people, a bird from the Miocene, and Savannah insisting…. "I'll be right back, Mom!"

He rushed into his parents' room and found his sister sitting up in bed, having just woken.

"Savannah, do you *really* see dinosaurs?"

She nodded. Then she looked out of the window and said, "But I don't see any now."

He ran back to the kitchen just in time for his mother to place scrambled eggs at his place.

"No bacon?"

"Well," she began in an ominous drawl, "I was on my way to the grocery store after work yesterday when Mrs. Mason called and told me Melody had not come back to the ranch yet, and she asked if the three of you were at our house? She said she'd heard warnings about flash floods. When no one answered the phone at home, I knew there was reason to be concerned." Now his mother exploded with all the anger and fear Kevin realized had been stuffed inside her the day before. "I have never been so worried in all my life! You are old enough to look out for your little sister, even if Melody was being irresponsible—"

"She wasn't irresponsible!"

"You should have spoken up and insisted on going home earlier."

His mother had her hands on her hips now. She opened her mouth to say more, but behind her they heard Savannah say, "I just saw one."

"What, baby girl, what did you see?" his mother said, turning around and drawing Savannah into her arms.

"A dinosaur. It looked like a T-rex."

"Oh, help me, God!" Mrs. Sinclair gave up and went back to the stove. She added, "By the way Kevin, your father and I have agreed you are grounded until he comes home, with school the exception, of course. Melody is grounded, too, and she's had her cell phone taken away for a week."

For the next few days, Mrs. Bowersock came to babysit. Savannah told her all about the Clovis camp and had occasional fits when she cried for Mitzi. Kevin spent hours peering out of his bedroom window looking for the sign Davy had promised when the projectile point was ready. He wanted to call Melody and see how she was doing, but he was afraid to call on the ranch's landline in case Mr. or Mrs. Mason picked up first.

On Monday, Mrs. Sinclair waved Kevin and Savannah onto the bus. In honor of her first day in first grade Savannah was wearing her white shirt with the red heart held on by a sequin and matching red pants. Kevin chose his checked shirt and jeans, which reminded him of his journey to the Clovis camp and the quest for the projectile point. On his way to school Kevin decided to say nothing about it to anyone, but by the middle of the week when the excitement of beginning a new school year was beginning to die down he changed his mind.

He was happy to see his pals Aiden and Jacob again. He expected them to be just like Davy—a true friend if there ever was one. You could tell a friend anything, and he just had to believe you because he was your friend. During P.E. he pulled them aside.

"I have something to tell you," he said.

"Is it about a girl?" Aiden asked. Both boys giggled. Everyone knew Kevin had spent time with Melody Mason over the break.

"No," he said slowly. Something in their attitude made him change his mind. No one would believe he had seen ancient bison and camelops, learned to throw a spear and observed a mammoth hunt. On the other hand, he was somewhat of a celebrity because the three of them had survived the flash flood and Sombra had run away. The entire county was looking for the mare.

"I've got a Clovis projectile point," he said

instead. Well, he did not have it yet. Davy was making it for him, if he ever saw Davy again.

"What's a projectile point?" Jacob asked.

"It's a spear point."

"Oh, yeah. From Spear Point Ranch!" Aiden scoffed.

"My older brother said Melody's really hot," Jacob said.

In a flash, Kevin knew who Jacob's brother must be.

"They're not dating anymore," he said.

"Yeah, I know," Jacob said. "He dumped her. Maybe she's going steady with a caveman."

Kevin lunged at Jacob. He knocked him down so hard the wind went out of the other boy. As Jacob lay gasping on the ground, Aiden rushed to his defense and took a swipe at Kevin. Kevin stepped back to avoid the punch. Aiden kept spinning around with the force of his swing, but he lost his balance and fell. The boys lay on the ground in a tangled, surprised heap. The P.E. teacher ran up. He grabbed Kevin and Jacob by the arms and, yelling at Aiden to follow them, he escorted the boys to the principal's office. Kevin wondered how Jacob had known about a caveman, and even after Jacob confessed to the principal what he had said to start the fight, he still didn't know.

The principal gave them a stern warning that their behavior was unacceptable on the school campus. He dismissed Jacob and Aiden but told Kevin to stay because he wanted to talk to him. Before he could begin, one of Kevin's classmates came in to give the principal a note. The principal excused himself and said he would be right back. The girl, who had glasses and braces, leaned close and whispered, "Did you really see a caveman?"

Startled, Kevin said, "Why do you ask?"

"My little sister and your little sister are in the same class at Murray Springs Elementary. Cavemen are all Savannah talks about. Well, that and dinosaurs, too."

This girl had once complimented Kevin on his artwork and he thought he could trust her.

"Yes, I did see a caveman, but actually they're called Clovis—"

The girl hooted so suddenly that spit flew between her teeth and hit him on the nose. After she ran out of the room, he could hear her laughter bouncing off the metal lockers in the hallway. He reached for a tissue and was wiping his face when the principal returned.

"There's no need to cry, Kevin. I'm not going any further with this. I know you're having it tough with your dad being away, but you're not the only kid without a dad at Fort Huachuca, or a mom for that matter. Your classmates will forget about this caveman thing when the next exciting story comes along."

"I'm not crying, sir," Kevin said, but he was so

miserable now he did want to cry. And the principal was wrong. Kids really did remember these things. Forever.

The principal called his mother to pick him up. After he explained to his mother why he had been in the principal's office Kevin said, "You've got to tell Savannah not to blab. Everyone in school is teasing me."

"Well, then, you shouldn't go making up stories."

Kevin huffed into his shirt collar, but he had to admit it was his fault. Savannah was only six years old. He could not remember if he could keep a secret at her age. Melody had bought into it, too. After all, she had just broken up with her boyfriend and needed something to distract her. He was going to speak to Savannah. He would tell her that he had made it all up and to stop talking about the Clovis camp. It wasn't doing either of them any good for people to think they had been running around with ancestors of Native Americans.

When they got home, Kevin decided to wait for Savannah in her room until the bus dropped her off. As he looked around, he saw that Savannah had hung Irtyshi's necklace on her bedpost. He remembered what his mother had said to him the night of the flood about the shell looking old. When Irtyshi placed it over Savannah's head, it had been shiny and pink as if just plucked from the sea. Now as he peered closely at it, he saw it was scuffed and had lines of dust between its ridges. He also thought the sinew strap the shell hung on looked a little frayed. He had a feeling it would soon disintegrate, just as the leather bandage Berul had wrapped over the cut on his palm did.

When Savannah finally burst into her bedroom she was full of tales from first grade, and Kevin changed his mind. He did not want to risk bringing up the Ice Age world, which might start her talking about it again. Their encounter with people from 13,000 years ago was over. He had to accept that. He did not even bother to look out of his window for a sign the projectile point was ready before he went to bed.

Kevin woke earlier than usual for school, glad it was Friday and that he could look forward to the weekend. He could hear his mother's shower running, but he also thought he could hear something else. Yes, there it was again, a scratching noise at the backdoor.

Getting out of bed, he padded down the hall. He decided to look out of the window before opening the door. You never knew what could be making a noise like that in the desert—a roadrunner, a coyote, or a bobcat. To his astonishment, he saw Mitzi.

"She's home! Mitzi's home!" he shouted, unlatching the door. Then the significance of Mitzi's return struck him.

While Savannah and his mother fussed and cooed over the dog, Kevin plotted how to get back to the

Clovis camp. He decided he would have to risk contacting Melody.

At one point his mother sat back and said, "I think Mitzi's gained weight. She must have been staying with someone. It's odd that whoever it was didn't call us because our phone number is on her nametag."

"They don't have phones, Mom," Savannah said. "Ow! Kevin hit me!"

"Children, don't fight. It's a happy day. Mitzi's back and your father will be home soon, too." She put her arms around their shoulders. "I'm going to ask you to do something for me. I want you to be good for a couple of hours by yourselves tomorrow morning while I drive to the airport in Tucson."

Their mother always went alone to pick up their father, saying it was like a date to get to know each other again.

"I'm leaving at nine o'clock. Mrs. Bowersock has a hair appointment and can't get here until eleven," she continued. "Can you do that for me? Behave yourselves?"

"Yes, Mom," they said in unison.

After school Kevin waited until his mother and Savannah were in the backyard playing ball with Mitzi to call the Masons, not caring who answered the phone. Fortunately, it was Melody.

"Mitzi's back!"

"So?"

"Don't you see? It's the sign Davy told us about. It means the spear point is ready!"

"Well, why doesn't Tom bring it back then? He's been to your house before."

"Remember Melody, he helped us escape and Rescalispel was mad. Who knows what's happened to Tom and Davy since we've been there."

"Kevin, I have been in so much trouble, I don't even want to talk about it. The obsidian point is still gone. Those stupid projectile points mean so much to Dad."

She sounded like she was going to cry.

"Melody, we have to go back to get it!"

"When? And how? I'm grounded, you know."

"For how long?"

"Mom said until the projectile point reappears. Dad believes me when I say I didn't take it, but Mom remembers seeing you and me by the display case, and she knows I know where the key to it is kept. She won't agree to sign my driver's permit until it's back."

Kevin knew this was really bad news for kids who were going to turn sixteen soon.

"I've had an idea," he said. "My mom is going to Tucson to pick up Dad tomorrow. She's leaving at nine and Mrs. Bowersock is coming at eleven. That gives us two hours to get to the Clovis camp and back."

"Are you crazy? That's not enough time. I don't

have a horse anymore. Between the three of us, we have one working bicycle."

"We've got to go soon, Melody! I'm sure Davy and Tom will set off before long with their aunt and mother for New Mexico. Remember?"

Melody was quiet a moment, then she said, "My parents are going to Nogales tomorrow morning to look at some cattle Dad's thinking of buying. I said I would go with them, but I'll get out of it. Call me when your mother leaves for the airport."

TWENTY

TIME GETS OUT OF CONTROL

"REMEMBER, you promised to be good until Mrs. Bowersock arrives, and while she's here, too."

Kevin nodded yes at his mother. Maybe if he did not speak an untruth out loud he would not feel so guilty.

As soon as the car pulled away, Kevin made his phone call, and then he said to Savannah, "Get dressed!"

"Where are we going?"

"To the Clovis camp, one last time."

"But we're not supposed to leave the house."

"We'll be there and back before anyone knows we've been gone. Hurry!"

"I don't want to go. I'm afraid!"

"You've got to come with us. I can't leave you alone."

"Who's us?"

"Melody's coming, too."

Melody's name motivated Savannah, and in record time she was ready and asking him to tie her shoes. Unlike Mitzi, Kevin had lost weight over the past couple of weeks and his jeans were threatening to slide to his knees. He went to his room and grabbed the first belt he could find, the one Mrs. Bowersock had given him.

In less than five minutes they heard a car pull into the driveway. Melody was at the wheel of the old four-door sedan Kevin remembered seeing under the blue tarp by the barn. Like Mr. Mason's tractor, the car had been kept in mint condition over the years.

"Brad learned to drive in this and I did, too," she said.

"I didn't know you already knew how to drive," Kevin said, admiringly.

"Every kid who grows up on a ranch knows how to drive by the time they can see over the dash. Buckle up, Savannah!"

Melody was very careful to keep to the speed limit on the highway to Moson Road, and then she drove a little faster to the turnoff for the Clovis site.

"Oh darn," she said as she parked the car. "It's Mr. Griggs."

The volunteer guide ambled over to them.

"Coming for a tour with the kiddoes, Melody? Say, I've seen you before," he said to Kevin. "What's your name, son?"

"Kevin Sinclair, sir. And this is my sister Savannah."

"Sinclair? Like that oil company with a brontosaurus for its mascot?"

"I've seen one," Savannah piped up.

Mr. Griggs winked at Kevin.

"Let's go on our hike," Melody said as she locked the car and pocketed the keys as if she had been driving legally for years.

"And where might you be going?" Mr. Griggs asked.

"To the Clovis camp," Savannah said.

"Well, you've certainly come to the right place. Watch out for mammoths!"

"Oh, we will," Savannah replied as Melody and Kevin each took a hand and hurried her toward the entrance.

"Be careful going into that arroyo," Mr. Griggs called after them. "The footholds were washed away by the last flood. Say aren't you the kids they were looking for recently? The kids they thought might have drowned?"

Not looking back, the children sprinted ahead. They slid down the path where it dropped into the arroyo and turned right, then left, the black mat spinning out beside them like a thread into the labyrinth of time. The striated prehistoric soils in the cliff below it began to fall, and suddenly their heads popped up into the Pleistocene. The weather could not have been more opposite to the warm and sunny Arizona climate they had just left in the twenty-first century. Lightning flashed on the horizon again. Storm clouds piled on top of each other, thick and angry, and underneath them the air blew cold. Kevin scanned the wide valley for ancient bison and camelops herds.

Melody stumbled and flung out her hands to break her fall. Then she began to shriek.

"Melody, shut up!" Kevin said. "We'll have every saber-tooth cat in the area stalking us for dinner!"

"Look! Hoofprints!"

"They have to be Sombra's," Kevin said, peering at the large, round indentations in the dried mud. "The only horses here are Equus occidentalis. They're singled-toed, too, but they're only about the size of ponies and their hoofs aren't so big."

"If Sombra made it this far, she might still be alive."

They hurried in the direction of the Clovis camp. No one was waiting for them at the grassy mound as Kevin had hoped. Who knew how many days had passed in the Ice Age, even though Mitzi had appeared only yesterday? Possibly Tom and Davy had given up, if they were still alive. After all, they had last seen the brothers surrounded by a mob. He began to feel a little uneasy. Who knew what waited ahead of them?

"Maybe we should go home," he said.

"Nonsense. I want to see if Sombra's at the camp. She has a good instinct for going back to a place she's been before. Remember when we found the bones of the ground sloth in the stream bank? She knew where she was then."

Melody took the lead.

They paused at the mammoth kill site and saw to their amazement that most of the dead animal remained, as if the tribe had left camp in a hurry, not bothering to process the meat for traveling. One of the cow's hind legs had been dragged up to her head; Kevin didn't see the other one. The carcass had attracted flies and small scavengers that scurried into the bushes under the trees. The waterhole had dried up. It had been a shallow one, Kevin recalled, but the water disappearing so quickly made him think that more time had passed in the Pleistocene than only a little over a week on his side of history.

He picked up a broken spear shaft straightener crafted from bone similar in appearance to the relic on display at the San Pedro House; it must have been stepped on by a mammoth to sustain such damage. He put it back where he had found it, remembering Mr. Mason's admonition to let artifacts remain in place. Now he knew for sure the dead mammoth was Big Eloise. Thirteen millennia later, the mammoth and the spear shaft straightener would be discovered at this very spot.

They ran on to the camp. It was deserted. Naked

branches lay like scattered matchsticks where once the houses had stood, the brush that stuffed them blown away like tumbleweeds. The hearths were dark with charcoal, and a few broken gourds lay around them. The ramada was still there, but most of the roof had collapsed, the leaves shrunken and brown, as much without life as the mammoth. A blast of wind raised billows of dust, and for a moment, it looked as if the camp were populated by ghosts. Rescalispel's house was the only one still standing, recognizable by the juvenile mammoth tusks at the entrance.

They heard the long, plaintive call of a dire wolf. Savannah clutched Melody around her legs and buried her face in them. Kevin could feel the shift in atmospheric pressure and recalled what Davy had said about the dire wolf's howl indicating rain would come soon.

"We should go back," Kevin said again, his mother's warning ringing in his ears that he was old enough to insist on going home. "I don't see Tom and Davy or Sombra, either. Everybody is gone. We're too late."

"Wait," Melody said. "I'm going to try something." She put her fingers in her mouth and whistled. It was a loud and piercing sound that would travel far.

A few minutes passed without anything happening except for the storm moving toward them. The clouds they had seen earlier rose up like great gray towers. Kevin took a deep breath of the electric air and felt an exhilarating sense of being alive. He wanted to stay alive. He announced, "We're going!"

At that moment they heard a whinny. Sombra appeared on the other side of the deserted camp with Davy and Tom on her back. The saddle was missing, but the bridle remained. Davy had his hands on the reins and was wearing Melody's rodeo hat. Tom rode behind him, holding his spear.

"Sombra!" Melody cried, shaking Savannah free. She ran toward the horse, which was glistening with sweat as if she had come galloping from a distance. The boys slipped off. The mare lowered her head and made soft, rumbling sounds in Melody's arms.

"Where is everyone?" Kevin asked. In reply, Davy put his hand up, palm out, in the classic gesture for caution. They turned to watch Tom stalk Rescalispel's house, spear at the ready. Kevin instinctively reached for Savannah's hand. Tom went inside and came out soon after. He was holding Rescalispel's necklaces.

"He hasn't been here for a while, but I can't believe he's gone for good. He wouldn't have left these."

Kevin remembered the necklaces from the first time he had seen Rescalispel. He knew they were valuable in this culture.

Melody had finished inspecting Sombra from the tips of her ears to her tail. She tied the horse to a tree and joined them, wearing a thoughtful expression.

"Is everything OK with Sombra?" Kevin asked.

"She's fine, but something's curious. Her hooves need trimming. We had the farrier over just before I started babysitting you and Savannah, which was only about three weeks ago, believe it or not, back there." Melody nodded toward the arroyo. "We asked him to take her shoes off because I wasn't riding in competitions anytime soon. But I would say there's two months' growth on her hooves where we stand now in Tom's world. Hooves are like fingernails, they keep growing and you have to file them back every so often. And her mane and tail are longer than I remember. Ask Davy how long they have been waiting for us."

Davy had followed some of this conversation. He said, "Our mother and sister left with Irtyshi and our cousins along with most of our father's clan over two moons ago. The others stayed with Rescalispel for a while. Rescalispel was sure you would return because he knew you would come back for the obsidian spear point. He hoped you would bring Savannah. In the end, Rescalispel's people grew tired of waiting and left him. They decided to go south, following the mammoth herd. Game around here has been scarce. The waterhole dried up, as you can see. It is doubtful the mammoths will ever come back."

"Why didn't you go with Irtyshi?" Melody asked.

"To'meh promised to give you the spear point to give to your father." Davy appeared a little surprised at the question. It was a principle of honor, after all. He looked at his brother, who took it out of his pouch and handed it to Melody. Davy said, "I have fixed it almost as good as the day it was knapped!"

Indeed, Kevin could not tell where Davy had flaked the point to correct the damage. He wondered if Mr. Mason would notice the difference.

Tom took the projectile point back from Melody and returned it to the pouch. Then he leaned over and tied the pouch to her belt. His fingers accidentally brushed her shirt and Melody blushed. Tom appeared embarrassed, and both of them looked away from each other. Kevin and Davy shared a smile.

"Where have you been all this time?" Kevin asked him.

"We found a hiding place half a morning's walk away, but since Sombra showed up, we can get back to camp in less time than it takes to skin a cat!"

The brothers thought this was a good joke. Kevin thought it sounded like something Mrs. Bowersock would say. For a weird moment, he wondered if the boys had grown up with an early version of the babysitter in the Clovis camp.

"At least you didn't eat Sombra," Kevin commented.

"That's not funny," Melody said, glowering at him.

"What happened to Slats?" he asked to change the subject.

"He went with the clans who travel after the mammoths," Davy replied, indicating Mexico.

"He didn't stay with his father?" Then Kevin remembered how Rescalispel had slapped his son and knocked him down the night of the flood in the arroyo. He didn't blame him.

"What will you do now? Melody asked.

"We will join Irtyshi," Tom said. He mumbled another sentence and fell silent.

Up to now, Kevin had understood everything Tom had said, which he thought remarkable, but then the old confusion set in, just as it had in the past when Tom's emotions jumbled his speech, like static breaking up a radio transmission.

Davy explained, "Our aunt's clan was so impressed with To'meh's performance at the mammoth hunt that they have elected him heir to their headman, Irtyshi's husband. To'meh did not want to accept this position because Chukotka is his son, but Chukotka was relieved because he wants to be a shaman, not a spear thrower. When he was nine, the spirits reached out to him in a vision. He began to sing the praises of nature. Our own shaman is teaching him to cure the sick with plants. Now he can focus on his calling. To'meh made it clear he had promised to wait for you before we followed them, but we have a long journey ahead. We know the way to the crossroads because it is foretold."

"What do you mean?"

"The way is passed down through stories…"

"…told around the campfires," Kevin said, finishing the sentence. He had a feeling the crossroads were a way of saying trade routes, judging by the seashells and other items not native to southern Arizona.

"From there, Irtyshi will take another course to her destination."

"Is this foretold, too? I mean, do you have directions how to get there?"

Davy shook his head.

"Some routes are secret to protect hunting grounds and waterholes," he said, "like the flesh of the fruit protects the seed. Once exposed, you get this."

Taking his knife, Davy slashed open a gourd, one of several still intact at the campsite. The gourd's seeds spilled on the ground and were immediately quarreled over by small rodents with widespread eyes and pointed ears, the ugliest rats Kevin had ever seen. He hoped their species had died out in the great Pleistocene extinctions of North America, but he thought perhaps their descendants were still living in urban centers, such as New York City.

"Irtyshi travels with at least fifty kinfolk. No other tribe will harm such a crowd. But two boys? It is a perilous journey for us. If the clans we meet are not friendly, we are doomed." He mentioned hunger, thirst, dire wolves, and bad weather as other dangers.

"It is important for us to reach our aunt as soon as possible."

"We are fearless! No man or beast will harm us!" Tom said as if to inspire bravado in both himself and his brother. He frowned fiercely and jumped about with his spear.

Davy did not look convinced, Kevin thought. In fact, he looked as if he felt sick to his stomach. Two months' head start would probably mean the tribe had covered a considerable distance. They would be many miles ahead of them by now.

Melody, of course, had understood very little of the conversation and looked inquiringly at Kevin. He summed up what Davy had told him, after which she went over to Sombra, put her arms around her neck and whispered in her ear. The horse paid attention and nodded her head.

While Tom walked around the camp a second time, making sure Rescalispel did not return for a surprise appearance, Davy took the opportunity to explain to Kevin that the jasper projectile point he had been knapping for him had been mislaid during the rumpus after the mammoth hunt celebration.

"Thank you, anyway," Kevin said. He supposed it was a good thing the jasper point had disappeared. How would he explain to his mom and dad that he was in possession of a prehistoric artifact? They would surely ask him where he found it and make him turn it in. An old shell was one thing, but a highly identifiable Clovis projectile point was another.

Davy's generosity made him want to give Davy something in return, but he could not think of anything he had with him except his baseball cap, and Davy seemed happy with Melody's rodeo hat. He had not even brought his backpack with him, which Davy might have appreciated. Then he noticed Davy looking at his waist. That was it! He undid the buckle and took off the belt.

"Here," he said.

"Oh," was all Davy could say as he took the belt with its silver and turquoise decoration. He held it like a sacred object.

"Let me show you how it works," Kevin said. He fastened the belt around Davy's waist, took it off and had Davy do it himself. Davy did a little dance. Kevin joined him and then almost fell down as his pants slid to his knees. The boys laughed uproariously, after which Davy took a length of sinew from several he had wrapped around his arm and drew it through the loops on Kevin's pants, making sure to tie it securely in the front.

Tom finished scouting for trouble. All this time Savannah had been making daisy chains from prehistoric flowers and had grown restless. When she pointed at the deserted camp Tom nodded and said in Clovis it was permissible to explore. Kevin watched her run off, thinking it was time they went home instead, which would be much quicker than coming as now they could ride Sombra to the arroyo.

He was about to suggest this when he saw Tom join Melody by the horse. They had a conversation which was mostly pantomime, after which Melody handed the reins to Tom and turned away to wipe her eyes with her sleeve. Then she straightened up like a soldier and marched over to Kevin.

"I've decided to give Sombra to Tom and Davy," she said. "If they ride, they'll be able to outdistance any person on foot and hopefully escape any wolves and saber-toothed cats they meet along the way. With any luck, they'll reach Irtyshi at the crossroads before she leaves to rejoin her husband's clan. I couldn't bear to think we had cost them their lives just because they stayed to wait for us and we didn't come sooner.

"I need to do something before we leave," she added. "I want to tell Tom and Davy how to take care of Sombra, and I need you to translate."

Melody started with basic equine facts and what to do if complications arose such as colic, where the horse's gut expanded, which should be treated by reduced food intake and walking sessions. It was also important to file Sombra's teeth periodically, which was called floating, to keep them level because uneven teeth could cause painful chewing issues. She showed them how to trim her hooves, but she appeared perplexed about how they would do this until Davy piped up and said he could fashion something for Sombra's teeth and hooves by the description of the tools Melody was giving him. She illustrated how to pick up Sombra's feet and check them for abscesses, or how if the hoof was hot she might go lame and this was called founder, and if untreated she could die from it. Kevin had no idea taking care of a horse was so complicated. He wondered how they ever survived in the wild.

Tom's eyes were a little glassy when Melody finished, but Kevin had no doubt that between the brothers they would remember the important points.

Savannah had found two of her little dolls that had been left behind and was playing by herself on the scraps of mat under what was left of the ramada. Lightning flashed in the distance, followed by a rumble of thunder. She jumped up in fright, dropping the dolls, and ran to join them. Everyone agreed it was time to go. The impending storm, another one to appear during the monsoon season in their separate worlds, gave them a sense of urgency.

As Tom and Davy prepared to mount Sombra, Melody said, "Wait, Kevin. I want to do one more thing."

"You always want to do one more thing, and it's making us late," Kevin grumbled. Girls didn't change much as they grew older, he thought. Melody could dilly-dally just like Savannah. He was also worried that Mrs. Bowersock, who had taught him that word, might be waiting at their house by now.

"Where we come from, when we say good-bye to someone we care about we give them a kiss," Melody said to Tom. She leaned forward and placed her lips on his mouth. Then everyone had to kiss each other, including Savannah, which further delayed them. By the time the boys had mounted and were riding to the east, leaving in a grand gallop, rainclouds were sliding over the mountains to the west.

They had taken a few steps toward the arroyo when Savannah pointed in front of them and said, "I see them! The dinosaurs!"

"Those are just clouds, Savannah," Kevin said, but he had to admit that if he used his imagination they did resemble dinosaurs, an Apatosaurus and a T-rex. He would have liked to have seen a stegosaurus, which was his favorite.

Savannah suddenly looked distracted.

"Wait!" she cried. "I forgot my dolls!" She turned and ran back toward the ramada.

He whirled around to grab his sister but before he could, Melody placed a hand on his arm. She said in a whisper, "Kevin, look."

TWENTY-ONE
THE THUNDER LIZARD

THE DESERTED CAMP was deserted no longer. A smaller number of Clovis people than before populated it, but fires were lit, a few of the houses appeared occupied and the ramada was intact, although the green leaves that formed its canopy were on their way to turning brown.

"I don't see Irtyshi or Chukotka, or the elder who taught me to throw a spear," Kevin said. "Zahn and his parents are gone, too. These are Rescalispel's followers, who are waiting for Savannah. They haven't left yet. *We've gone in-between!*"

Savannah was standing in the middle of the camp in front of another little girl as she traded her dolls for Snow White's slippers, the pair she had lost.

"We've got to get out of here. I don't see Tom or Davy, either, but they must be nearby, still waiting for us. Whistle for Sombra again!"

Melody raised her hands to her mouth, but her lips had gone dry and her fingers trembled. She could not make a sound. Then from behind, brown hands fell on their shoulders. Slats held Kevin in a tight grip, and another boy grasped Melody. They forced them toward the crowd of tribespeople, which had formed a circle around Savannah. The tribespeople were now squatting down, as if waiting for something to happen. The boys pushed Kevin and Melody to their knees and sat behind them. The little girl who had exchanged Snow White's slippers for the dolls fled.

Rescalispel strutted up to Savannah. Every fiber in Kevin's body screamed this was wrong. He started to stand up, preparing to fling himself at Rescalispel, but Slats pushed him back down. The Clovis boy shouted, "My father is headman! You cannot deny him!"

Savannah's face expressed her terror, and she sank as low to the ground as she could. Rescalispel's hands hovered over her head. The allure of the color and softness of her golden tresses was irresistible to him, just as it had been to the women and children who had played with it on the day of the mammoth hunt. Suddenly her hair sprang up to his fingers like magic, and the crowd around them gasped.

"See what powers I have!" he bellowed. "I will take this child into my household and she will bring us good fortune as has been prophesized!"

Rescalispel's eyes darted to the Storyteller, who

had not left with the brothers' aunt. The Storyteller nodded his head and looked around the crowd with glee.

"It has been foretold! It has been foretold!" he cackled as Savannah's hair swirled higher and higher.

Melody crept over to Kevin, her captor having released her because he was enraptured by the display in front of them and, like so many of the tribe, had raised his hands from her shoulders in a gesture of awe. Her own hand found Kevin's, and she held onto it so tightly he almost had to ask her to let go of it. He knew he had to do something.

"Slats," he pleaded, talking over his shoulder. "Don't let your father take my sister."

"You brought her back to my world," he growled. "And for that I have paid with this!"

Slats relaxed his grip slightly, giving Kevin enough mobility to turn and look at him. The boy had an ugly scar healing on his cheek under his left eye. He remembered how Slats had defied his father to warn them Rescalispel was coming to kidnap Savannah the night of the mammoth hunt.

"*Thank you,*" Kevin said.

The angry V of Slats' eyebrows relaxed like dove's wings and his lips parted slowly as if he was about to speak, but at that moment they heard the tribespeople call out in wonder, and both boys turned to see what was going on in front of them.

Wisps of Savannah's hair danced like dervishes

around Rescalispel's hands. He spread his fingers in a dramatic gesture as if teasing it higher, playing with the tribespeople to convince them it was in his power to do this. As if in emphasis, lightening flashed above their heads. Suddenly Kevin knew it was not enchantment that caused Savannah's hair to leap about, but the energy generated by the approaching storm, such as he had felt earlier. He had learned about this effect in science class. Savannah's fluffy hair did not have the weight to counteract the stimulus. As the headman's fingers disappeared into the golden mass, she began to shriek. At that moment, a wind blew into the camp with a roar like a giant beast. People screamed as fires snuffed out, houses popped open, and a foul odor enveloped them.

"Go!" Slats cried suddenly. "And this time do not come back!"

Rescalispel's son released Kevin and pushed him away. Dragging Melody with him, Kevin lunged toward Savannah. As surprised as everyone else at the chaos surrounding them, the headman was looking around. Taking advantage of his distraction, Kevin snatched Savannah from under his hands. In the next heartbeat, thunder boomed. The ground trembled like a hundred earthquakes so that if the children had not been clutching each other they would have been thrown apart. Then above the dust and mayhem a reptilian head on a long neck appeared. The head rotated slowly so that a huge eye was looking down on the fleeing crowd. Kevin stopped in awe.

"Apatosaurus!" he said.

"Kevin, come on!" Melody cried, pulling at him.

He took a few steps, but he had to have one last look. As he did, he saw Rescalispel running toward them, weaving between the huge dinosaur's legs, his head easily fitting under the giant's belly. He did not know if he should be more afraid of the man or the apatosaur.

They ran through the alley of trees still sporting patches of whitewashed symbols, which as they passed began to waver like mirror images in a funhouse. The ground started to swell and plunge in disorienting waves, and it was difficult to stay on their feet, but they managed to keep going. They passed Big Eloise and the dried-up water hole, and then the land began a steep decline and they were running downhill with such momentum they could not stop. Finally, the angle eased and they slowed enough to be able to look around.

Where once the grassy plain had opened before them now stretched an expanse of groves of palm-like trees and shallow lakes surrounded by wide muddy beaches. The atmosphere was warm and humid, and the vegetation lush and jungle-like. Swirls of moss covered the ground with brilliant green fan-like ferns poking through. The grassy mound was gone and Kevin had no idea where the arroyo was, if it existed at all. Looking down, he saw footprints twice and three times the size of the mammoth footprints at Murray Springs. Turning around, he saw Rescalispel was still behind them.

The headman had stopped, too, appearing as astonished as they were by the new surroundings. He clutched his chest, bare of necklaces, which seemed to disturb him more that discovering he was in another time period. He glared at Kevin as if this were all his doing, then he shifted his glance to Savannah. Rescalispel had not brought his spear, but he did have a knife in his belt, which he took out and brandished menacingly. They could not just stand still and wait for him, so they sprinted through a patch of jungle, hoping the trees draped with clinging vines would hide them. A great roar brought them to a halt and they whipped around.

Out of the jungle between them and Rescalispel stepped a ferocious-looking dinosaur with a long tail, walking on powerful back legs and ducking its head low to skim under the trees. Bony horns protruded over its yellow eyes, giving it a devilish appearance. Its jaws clapped open and shut in anticipation of a good meal; the children could hear the snaps from yards away.

"A T. rex!" Savannah cried.

"It's not a T. rex," Kevin said squinting at it. "The arms on a T. rex are small and mostly useless. This one's got longer arms to hold its prey while it tears it apart to eat it, and it hunkers over a little, see? It's an allosaur."

"We're going to die!" Savannah moaned.

"No we're not," Melody said. "Rescalispel is."

The massive carnivore had turned toward the Clovis man, who had not anticipated anything coming out of the trees and had almost run into it. He fell beneath the theropod as a three-toed foot with sharp claws as long and curved as bananas came down on top of him. Rescalispel screamed. Kevin put his hands over Savannah's eyes. Suddenly the screaming stopped as the allosaur tore Rescalispel apart with its dexterous hands, after which it gulped a good portion of him. Savagely shaking its head, it sent what was left of the headman flying over the late Jurassic palm trees and out of sight.

It dawned on Kevin why Rescalispal had been gone the last time they had seen Tom and Davy at the camp: he had stumbled into the Jurassic world with them, leaving his followers behind to later go south without him. One hundred fifty million years from now a researcher with a wide-brimmed hat, brush and sieve would uncover the necklaces abandoned in his Pleistocene house and the mammoth tusks at its door.

The children turned and crept away through the jungle grove. They emerged a short while later onto an open plain studded with grass and small tree-like ferns around lakes reflecting the periwinkle blue of the sky. The pink and orange mountains in the distance looked familiar and the valley did, too. They were still in Arizona not far from Spear Point Ranch, but they might as well have been looking at an ocean without a boat, so vast were the epochs of time they had to cross to get home.

To the left, grazing on the lower branches of conifers was a small group of dinosaurs with plates on their backs and four spikes on their tails.

"Stegosaurs!" Kevin exclaimed. He had seen what he had wished for. He opened his mouth to tell them more about these herbivores, but Melody interrupted him before he could say anything.

"I think I know the way home," she said. "Those are the Mule Mountains. I see them every day. That means the arroyo can't be far away."

To their dismay, they heard a great crashing in the jungle. Motivated to keep going, they ran in the direction Melody indicated but had not gone far when Savannah tripped and skinned her knees. Out of breath, she crumpled on the ground.

"Melody, wait!" Kevin called, kneeling by his sister. "You have to get up!"

"I can't. I'm tired. And I'm thirsty." Her eyes filled with tears. "I really did see dinosaurs, didn't I?"

"Yes, you did. But if we don't get out of here fast, you're going to get eaten by one just like Rescalispel!" Kevin did not want to be mean, but he needed to impress on his sister how urgent it was to flee.

Melody ran back to them.

"I've found the way, I'm sure of it. Ahead there's a deep ditch about where the arroyo would be near the Clovis dig. Savannah, you can ride piggyback," she said, helping the little girl up. "Hold tight."

They heard branches snapping and footsteps slogging through mud. There it was again, the fleet-footed, meat-eating dinosaur emerging from the jungle oasis. In another moment, the allosaur had seen them and was running swiftly toward them on agile legs with tail outstretched. Horrible snorts exploded from its nose and rumbles burst from its throat. The allosaur was still hungry, Kevin thought. Rescalispel had been only a snack. The wind blew from behind the beast and sent a nauseating odor of stale meat and blood toward them.

Even carrying Savannah, Melody was faster than Kevin, and she soon outdistanced him. Savannah clung to her back like a monkey, screeching like one, too. The allosaur overtook Kevin, but he strode purposefully onward. Kevin realized it was after the girls and had not noticed him; the commotion Savannah made had attracted his attention instead. He saw that Melody would reach the crack in the earth she had told him about before the allosaur reached her, so he threw himself behind a boulder and watched. Just in time, Melody arrived at the opening and jumped into it with Savannah. The girls disappeared from view.

The dinosaur pranced around above them, but the

opening was far too narrow to admit it. The creature's arms were made for ripping and tearing, not digging, and it became frustrated at its inability to reach them. The ditch appeared to be only eight to ten feet long, as if it was the tip of a massive faultline. The allosaur cocked its head and peered into it, reminding Kevin of a robin seeking an earthworm. There was no way he could slip under the nose of the dinosaur to jump in and join the girls. He would have to wait his chance.

As he crouched behind the rock assessing his next move, he discovered he was thirsty, even though the air around him was so humid it made his shirt stick to his back. Savannah had said she was thirsty, too, but he could not see any clear bodies of water nearby in his Jurassic surroundings, or mountain springs in front of him. He thought what a great invention a water bottle was and wondered if he would ever see one again.

The dinosaur was still preoccupied with the girls, which reassured Kevin they must be waiting for him to return to the future. Encouraged, he slunk from fern to fern to dwarfish, palm-like tree until only a bare mossy patch separated him from the allosaur. At that moment, the dinosaur swung its head around looking for other prey and saw the stegosaurs Kevin had spotted earlier. The adults were about the size of a small bus; the young were no bigger than good-sized sheep, which meant they had only recently hatched. The allosaur turned and charged.

Taking his chance, Kevin scooted to the fault and dropped in. He did not fall very far. The edge was only a few feet above his head.

"Let's go!" he said.

Melody gave him one of her sarcastic looks, the kind he did not want to see right now. Usually it meant something was wrong or completely unexpected. This time, it was both.

"This ditch won't lead us back to Murray Springs. In fact, it doesn't go anywhere. It's just a hole in the ground. While I was waiting for you with Mr. Stinky Breath hovering over us," Melody said in an accusing tone of voice, indicating she was exasperated he had taken so long to join them, as if he had been out for a stroll, not hiding from certain death, "I got to thinking we are meant to leave this place in time by going up, not down."

"What do you mean?"

"Think about it. When we left the twenty-first century to go to the Clovis world, we stayed just under the black mat. The Jurassic is much farther down. So, if you wanted to excavate something in the Jurassic world, you would need to dig *deeper* to get to it. I don't want to know what's below the Jurassic."

"It's the Triassic period, very dry with hot summers and cold winters. There weren't any polar ice caps at the time, and there was one supercontinent called Pangea. Reptile-like monsters roamed the earth—."

"And these aren't monsters?" Melody interrupted.

"Actually, Jurassic dinosaurs become our mammals and birds."

"Even birds?"

"Yes. Birds evolved from small, feathered dinosaurs that first walked on the ground before they evolved enough to fly."

"I don't want to go to the Tri- Tri- ," Savannah wailed, starting to scramble out of the fault.

At that moment, they heard frightened squeaks and the unmistakable roar of the allosaur. They peeped over the rim of the fault to see the small stegosaurus herd scatter in all directions, leaving a view of the allosaur facing off with the biggest member. The stegosaur's skin, like heavy-plated armor, protected him from the chomps of the allosaur's jaws. The upright plates along his back helped deflect the allosaur's claws from damaging his spine. Using his strong hips he swung his tail with its impressive spikes like a Norseman swinging four battle axes at once. One swipe hit its mark. The allosaur screamed as a spike lodged in its ribs. While the children watched, the stegosaur tried to dislodge its tail, but the spike had thrust deep. The stegosaur thrashed about until finally the spike broke off in the theropod. The allosaur dropped to the ground, bleeding copiously. With his low-slung head, the stegosaur examined his enemy. It had been a lucky strike. The allosaur was fatally injured.

The children helped each other out of the fault. They watched the stegosaurs regroup and move away, the little ones trotting along on their short legs as fast as they could to keep up. The allosaur lay twitching in its death throes. Then a shadow moved over the ground. Kevin looked up to see a prehistoric winged reptile glide over the prone dinosaur. It had a long, narrow beak, extended neck, leathery wings about three feet long and a very short tail. When it landed near the allosaur it sat upright, using its claw-like hands attached to its wings to balance with its hind legs on the ground on all fours. Hunkered over, Kevin thought it appeared about as tall as he was. More shadows raked over them like a fleet of aircraft and soon a flock of ten ugly, featherless creatures surrounded the dead dinosaur.

"What are those?" Melody asked.

"They're pterodactyls," Kevin replied, rolling his eyes. Everyone knew what a pterodactyl looked like, he thought, even people who didn't know much about dinosaurs.

"I'm awfully thirsty. I wish we'd brought water," Melody said. "We need to find a way home soon."

They looked around. What appeared to be a path wound toward the mountains, which were not so far away as they had seemed before. They had run further than they realized. The time spent in the fault had given them a respite, so aside from feeling a need to drink, they were energized to go on. Again, Melody took the lead, and they ran toward the first rise in front of them. A little more than an hour later they paused to catch their breath and look around. The pterodactyls still dined on the allosaur, although not so many surrounded it as before. The stegosaurs had retreated out of sight. In the vast expanse, lakes sparkled and here and there were punctuated by the neck of an apatosaur, diplodocus or brachiosaur. Kevin could not see anything that appeared to be a way out of the Jurassic at the height where they had paused. He flopped down, followed by Melody and Savannah.

"These are your dinosaurs," he snapped at his sister. "You brought us here. Tell us how to get back."

Her face puckered up and her eyes filled with tears. She had hiked the mountain on her own steam and without complaint. Now he was sorry he had spoken so unkindly to her.

"Yes, think Savannah," Melody pleaded, but in a soothing tone like one she used to calm Sombra.

"I don't know how to get home," Savannah said, "but I do know I've lost Snow White's slippers again."

Melody was unconsciously fingering the pouch containing the spear point on her belt. Watching her, Kevin began to get an idea, not fully formed. An inkling, Mrs. Bowersock would have called it. He looked around. Many of the mountain peaks were still a long way above them. They could keep climbing. And then what? Throw themselves off one of them, hoping to land in Murray Springs by some miracle? Not all the tops of the mountains were as pointed as belfries. A few were rounded, rimmed with unhospitable, stony projections, without a clue to a window to the future. But one mountain, practically their neighbor, opened at its top like a bowl, and he could see from its nearer rim to the opposite side.

Kevin leapt to his feet. The girls got up slowly.

"Over there is an extinct volcano," he said. "At least I hope it's extinct. Anyway, what do you find around a volcano?"

"Don't play games, Kevin. I'm too tired," Melody said.

"Obsidian!"

"So?"

"Before I brought you to the Clovis camp, Tom and Davy took me to the San Pedro River to show me where their father died. There's a huge rock there, with bits of obsidian in it."

"Where you said you got that piece you showed me?"

"Yes, the one you didn't believe I brought back from the Pleistocene."

"OK, I believe you now. And?"

"Where do you find obsidian?"

The light bulb went on. Melody said, "Near a

volcano. I'd forgotten there was one next to the peak I recognized from the ranch."

"If we go over there," Kevin said, pointing to the sunken crater, "we will be closer to the Clovis camp."

"It's worth a try. Lead on!"

No longer climbing, they made good progress toward the volcano. They skirted the side of the mountain, to their left the rocky surface, to the right a steep drop. One more turn around this mountain and they would step foot on the volcano. Up ahead, wonderfully familiar, he saw the very rock where Tom and Davy's father had met his fate. He turned around to point it out, but he could see only Melody.

"Where's Savannah?"

"She was right behind me! She must have stopped along the way."

Melody pivoted carefully and retraced her steps, Kevin following. Not far back they came upon a flat ledge Kevin had passed without thinking, but Savannah had obviously had a look at it because there she stood, studying something. It was a primitive nest with four small, pink hatchlings inside. They huddled against each other amid chips of eggshells, bits of animal bones and the dusty rubble of the mountain. Savannah bent over them, enchanted with the creatures, which snapped their small beaks at her as if expecting to be fed. When food was not forthcoming, they raised their three-fingered bat-like hands in agitation, letting out piercing squeaks of distress.

Kevin realized these were pterodactyl offspring. As if in confirmation, they heard a flapping sound above them.

"C'mon, Savannah! We have to get out of here!" Melody said.

She bent over to grab Savannah's hand, but not before one of the hatchlings leaped up with surprising agility and clung to her belt. As it snapped its beak at her some of its tiny teeth pierced her jeans.

"Get it off! Get it off!" Melody shrieked, her cries echoing around the mountaintops.

Kevin took off his baseball cap and flapped it at the baby pterosaur. He finally dislodged it and watched as the hatchling tumbled down Melody's leg onto the ledge. They quickly retreated along the path to the volcano, finally reaching it and falling down behind a ridge where they huddled together.

Kevin opened his mouth to tell Savannah how stupid she was to stop at a pterodactyl nest, but suddenly he thought of his mother and how angry she got at him because she was worried about him when he did something irresponsible. He wondered if he would ever see her again, or if they would forever be entombed deep under the line of the black mat. Then he noticed it, or rather, he noticed the lack of it.

"Melody, where is the pouch with the spear point?"

She patted her waist all the way around and raised a horrified face to his.

"That little monster must have ripped it off!"

"We can't go back without it," Kevin said.

In spite of his determination to return the obsidian projectile point to Mr. Mason, everything inside him was telling him to leave it. The rock that was his clue to go forward in time was only a few minutes' walk away. Its pockets of volcanic glass reflected the sun as it began its descent to the west. He had not considered they might be spending the night in the Jurassic world. The air was already turning cool in the mountains and a breeze had come up. They did not have coats or sweaters; they had hiked above the tree line so there was no vegetation with which to build a shelter or huddle under. They were hungry and unbelievably thirsty. It was more important than ever to find their way home before dark.

"Listen!" Savannah said. "I hear someone calling my name!"

They were quiet a moment.

"I don't hear anything," Kevin said.

"It must be the wind," Melody added. "Or wishful thinking."

Not realizing he had made a decision until he stood up, Kevin announced, "I'm going back for the pouch. Melody, take Savannah to the rock up ahead and if I'm not back by dark, go home without me."

"Don't be crazy, Kevin. We don't even know if the rock will take us to Murray Springs. It could be, well, just another rock, like the fault was just a ditch."

But it wasn't just another rock, Kevin thought, remembering how Tom and Davy's father had tumbled from it to fight the saber-toothed cat and save their mother. He didn't feel at all courageous, but there was something inside him that was beginning to make his heart pump faster, a sort of determination that even as he stood there began to grow and lift his chest and clear his vision for the challenge ahead. Maybe this was how his father felt before combat, and he desperately wanted to get back to Murray Springs and ask him. As if in answer, the spirit of his Clovis friends' father assured him he would keep Savannah and Melody safe. Kevin did not know how he knew this, but there it was, making him bold. At the same time, he believed the magical powers the brothers were sure the obsidian spear point possessed would be enough for him.

After a few more protests, Melody agreed to go on with Savannah. Careful not to advertise the danger of his mission, Kevin kissed his sister on the cheek and promised to join her soon. His hand rested briefly on her head, on that golden hair that had brought them so much trouble. Then he turned to Melody. He decided kissing Melody would be awkward and gave her a thumbs-up instead.

When the girls were out of sight, he started back toward the pterodactyl nest. A few of them floated on drafts of air high over the ledge. He looked around for something to protect himself with. His cap would not be much defense against an adult pterodactyl, so he picked up a couple of fist-sized rocks and started for the nest.

The adults had seen him and began calling out to each other. Kevin hoped they were full from dining on the allosaur. When he reached the ledge he saw the pouch lying only inches away from the four hatchlings; the one that had jumped on Melody had rejoined its siblings. The baby pterodactyls cocked their heads and watched him creep toward the pouch. Just before he reached it, a large chunk of carrion dropped out of the sky and landed at his feet. Despite the blood and gore, he recognized the same brown scaly skin he had seen on the allosaur. The little pterosaurs were on it in an instant. Kevin saw his chance and lunged for the pouch, dropping one of the rocks the better to clutch it. As he turned to run, a great flutter of leathery wings made him duck his head. When he looked up, he found the hatchlings' parents had landed, one behind and one in front of him. They leaned over on their clawed hands and snapped their long beaks, looking craftily at him. The huge flying reptiles barred both exits to the path. He could not go forward to the volcano, or escape back to the Jurassic valley, had he wanted to.

The adult pterodactyls appeared puzzled about what to do with him. As he had guessed, they were gorged on meat and, like many animals when satisfied, saw no reason to continue eating. Even a zebra will walk past a lion when it is confident the lion has no interest in shopping for lunch. Some instinct acquired from his ancestors assured Kevin of this, but he was wary of the pterodactyls anyway. He did not think the ugly creatures would politely step aside, although it was worth a try with the one between him and the volcano.

"Excuse me, please."

In response to his voice, the pterodactyl dropped its eyelids halfway down, giving the impression of a lizard about to doze. This really could not be happening, Kevin thought hopefully. He took a step forward.

Suddenly the pterodactyl's eyes snapped open. Emitting a high-pitched squeak, it began walking toward him on the tips of its fingers and toes like a stiff-legged dog approaching a rival before a fight. Rather than taking a nap, the pterodactyl had been assessing what to do next. While the bird-like dinosaur was not hungry, Kevin knew he was close to its offspring and an unknown threat. Glancing quickly over his shoulder, Kevin saw the second pterodactyl doing the same thing.

"This sucks," he thought. He knew he had to do something, and fast.

Tucking the pouch inside his pants, he threw his remaining rock at the pterodactyl blocking the path to the volcano. The rock hit it in the chest. As it tottered and spread its wings for balance, Kevin snatched the meat from the hatchlings and tossed it over the side of the cliff. Shouting and jumping up and down and waving his cap above his head to make himself appear bigger, he charged the pterodactyl in front of him. Surprised, it vaulted into the air. At the same time, its mate left the cliff, soaring after what was left of the allosaur meat while the hatchlings raised a commotion about the abrupt departure of their meal. Other pterodactyls in the neighborhood had observed the disturbance and launched into the air. Soon their cries reverberated around the cliffs, making a tremendous din. In the uproar Kevin took off, racing toward the obsidian-studded rock.

When he reached the volcano he felt a tremendous heat coming from its surface accompanied by a growl from deep inside it. A plume of black steam shot into the sky and the inside of the crater began to glow reddish orange. *The volcano was about to erupt!* He ran toward the large rock, hoping to find the girls. They were not there, but their footprints went around it several times and did not lead away. They had vanished into thin air.

The volcanic mountain trembled, and the rock began to shake. He recalled it had come to rest by the San Pedro River, and he realized it was about to break free and roll away. To his surprise, Savannah and Melody tumbled down from on top of it. They tottered toward him on the bouncing mountain. They hadn't left him, after all, and were as confused as he was how the big rock would help them get home.

Then it was gone, careening downward. Where once the boulder had lain a gaping hole remained, and through this was a portal to the future. Like a telescope viewed back to front they saw ahead of them in miniature a grassy mound, a plain with oaks and willows bordering a river, and the arroyo.

They ran into the cone of the volcano through a tunnel of sparkling black rock illuminated from light cast into it from the Jurassic at one opening and the Pleistocene on the other. "Obsidian!" Kevin called out, but his voice was lost in the booms and pops surrounding them. The heat was almost unbearable. When they burst out of the mountain, they doubled over panting and feeling as if their lungs had been seared. In front of them, Kevin saw the familiar valley. Never had he been so glad to be in the Ice Age again.

"Did you get the spear point?" Melody asked when she caught her breath.

"Yes!" Kevin said, proudly waving the pouch above his head before he put it away again.

They knew the way back now, but they still had some distance to go. They had emerged near the river and took off immediately to the west toward the arroyo, ignoring their thirst that would have been slaked by the fast-flowing water. The boulder with its shiny black dots like a hundred eyes winked good-bye to them.

Unlike before, this Pleistocene was hot and dry,

more like the modern temperature he was used to in Murray Springs. Kevin had the impression they had moved forward in the epoch to the time when the lush vegetation had begun to shift to the semiarid climate, signaling the extinction of megafauna such as mammoths, saber-toothed cats and native horses. The dazzling blue lake was just a dot in the distance. Shallow impressions covered by what looked like algae dotted the plain, and Kevin realized he was looking at the origin of the black mat. By the time they reached the once-grassy mound, which to their relief was still there although now dotted with sparse brown shrubs, their lips were dry and the wind whipped dust into their eyes and mouths. Kevin could see Savannah teetering a little as she walked. She was much too parched to cry anymore.

"Let's rest a while," he said.

"I'm afraid if we stop now we won't get up again," Melody responded.

They staggered forward, each with an arm around Savannah. Soon they felt their feet jerking downward and their strides lengthening. To their great joy, they had stumbled on the entrance to the arroyo. Their footfalls became faster and even Savannah shook herself from her stupor and kept up with them, a gleam coming back to her eyes. They reached the sandy bottom of the arroyo; the line of the black mat in the striated walls rose above their heads. They were home! Well, almost home. A relic from the Pleistocene appeared before them.

"A tapir!" Kevin cried.

The mammal was dark brown with a lighter-colored head on which perched small round ears, making it look a little like a rhino with fur. The tapir stood at least three feet high at the shoulders and might have passed for a giant pig if it had not had longer legs and a short proboscis like an elephant's trunk. It also had an odd number of toes, three on the front and four on the hind feet. The tapir was as surprised to see them as they were to see her, because they realized a second later she was a female. Her baby walked out from between her legs, the only difference being the pale stripes lying horizontally along its torso, providing excellent camouflage.

"Oh," cooed Savannah and Melody together.

"Oh is right," Kevin said. "How are we supposed to get past *that*?"

The adult tapir was large enough to block their passage and appeared to be listening to something behind her. The calf was intrigued with the girls, as if it was not at all afraid of humans, and took a few confident steps toward them. Kevin began to get worried. He knew how protective parents could be. Just consider the pterodactyls!

Then suddenly they heard warning snarls. They looked up to see two huge dog-like creatures, one on each side of the arroyo. Each beast had the unmistakable posture of being poised to pounce with front legs spread, head down and tail at attention.

"Dire wolves!" Kevin cried, ready to turn around and run back to the Pleistocene, hopefully directly into the Clovis camp.

"Those aren't dire wolves. They're Wyatt and Earp!" Melody cried. As soon as she said their names, the dogs relaxed and wagged their tails. "We made it! We're back!"

"Then how do you explain the tapirs?"

"It's a conundrum," Savannah said with a grin.

The dogs leaped down and ran ecstatically to Melody, almost knocking her over. This frightened the tapirs, which turned back the way they had come and took off. Suddenly there was a shout and they heard a man cry, "I see them! They're here!"

Delighted, Kevin, Savannah and Melody waited for someone to appear, but no one did. After a moment it occurred to them the man had called out because of the tapirs. The dogs had trotted after them and now they were alone. In this moment the three of them felt the camaraderie of an adventure shared together. They had the scabs and torn clothes to prove it, the wicked thirst of being in the desert too long without water, Savannah's lost hat and slippers, Kevin's missing belt and Melody's runaway horse. They knew it was over. *So this is how the story ends,* Kevin thought, remembering his question to the Storyteller. He thought there never could have been a better ending than this, but as Mrs. Bowersock would say, he had something more up his sleeve, or in this case, tucked into his pants. He pulled out the pouch with the obsidian spear point and gave it to Melody. Then they all three collapsed in the sand.

TWENTY-TWO
EVERYTHING IN ITS PLACE

"Dad!"

"Dad!"

"Dad!"

It seemed like eons since Kevin had seen his father. In his arms he felt the stiffness of his uniform's fabric and smelled the bleach-like odor from its detergent mixing with the minty aroma on his cheeks. He did not need the scent of his father's shaving cream to know this was real.

"Have a drink," Sgt. Sinclair said, handing a water bottle to him and another to Savannah, who was clinging to his shirt.

"Kids should be prepared when they go for a hike in the desert," Mr. Griggs said, walking up. Then he added apologetically, "I should have called Bill Mason sooner when they didn't come back after an hour or two. The day got real hot."

"They're OK. That's what matters."

Melody was sitting on a cement bench near the entrance to the Murray Springs Clovis Site. All three of them had been faint and a little confused, and as a precaution, the local first responders had been called. After examining the children and concluding they were fine one of the EMTs said, "I've seen a lot of dehydration cases in the desert. Deliriums, too, where people babble just about anything, but in this situation, it's odd that each kid told the same story."

On their way to Mr. Mason's truck, they passed the old sedan.

"I wondered how you got here," Melody's father said, giving her a disapproving look because that is what a parent is supposed to do when a child disobeys, but it changed into a smile of love and relief. He turned his head away quickly after that, and Kevin thought he might be hiding tears. When he recovered he said, "You didn't see Sombra, did you? I told your mother you went to look for her."

Kevin looked at Melody, who was looking at him. Well, they had seen Sombra, but they had left her in the Pleistocene.

"The last place we were, she wasn't there," Melody replied.

At least that was true, Kevin thought.

"But we did find something else!"

They crowded around as Melody held out the pouch. It looked flat to Kevin, as if nothing was inside. Then the pouch began to disintegrate as if the leather was thousands of years old. In less than thirty seconds, there was only dust in her hands.

"Oh, oh, oh!" she said. "It was there, Dad! It was there."

Kevin had felt the hardness of the obsidian projectile point in the pouch next to his skin all through their last mad dash across the volcano and up until he had handed the pouch to Melody. *Where had it gone?* But Mr. Mason did not seem concerned. In fact, he got a twinkle in his eye.

"Dad," Melody asked as they got ready to leave, "What were tapirs doing in the wash?"

"They escaped from Mr. Lynch's ranch, the one he's turning into a big game preserve. It seems he applied for and received a permit to raise a herd. They're considered vulnerable on the endangered species list."

Sgt. Sinclair was going to drive the truck back to Spear Point Ranch, and Mr. Mason the old sedan. As Kevin climbed into the truck, he felt his pants slipping down. The length of sinew Davy had given him to tie up his jeans had disappeared like the pouch. It was a little awkward to hold onto his pants, but he was so happy he didn't care.

As the truck bounced down the dirt road away from the Murray Springs site, Kevin's dad reached into his pocket.

"Look what we found in a bush in the desert when we were looking for you."

"My hat!" Savannah said. "A camel knocked it off my head when we were going to the Clovis camp."

"Of course it did," Sgt. Sinclair said indulgently, and Kevin knew their mother had told their father everything.

When they pulled up to the Mason's house, Wyatt and Earp jumped out of the bed of the truck. Sgt. Sinclair said to Savannah, "Those two hounds remind me. What were you feeding Mitzi while I was gone? She's a little butterball."

"Mammoth meat," she said, and no one disagreed, not even Mrs. Mason or Kevin's mother, who had joined them.

Mr. Mason said to Kevin's father, "I know you're eager to take the children home, but I'd like to show Kevin and Melody something in the house. It won't take a moment."

Mrs. Mason took Kevin's parents and Savannah into the kitchen for a glass of lemonade. Kevin and Melody followed Mr. Mason over to the display case in the living room. They stared down at the shiny black spear point.

"When did this happen, Dad?" Melody whispered.

"Right before Griggs called me, just after I noticed the sedan missing from the barn. I came in here to check out the projectile points. I like to look at them when I have a lot of thinking to do, and I wanted to figure out where to find you. And there it was."

Kevin peered closer.

"Yes, something is different," Mr. Mason said, "Almost as if one side has been remodeled slightly? It would take a master artist to do it, I must say, and neither of you are flintknappers."

Mr. Mason waited for an explanation, but neither of them said a word. After a moment, Mr. Mason nodded his head as if everything had been concluded in a satisfactory manner, and that was the end of it.

A FEW DAYS LATER, Melody called.

"Sombra's coming home! A Border Patrol agent found her near the Arizona/New Mexico state line."

"How did he know who she belonged to?"

"Our brand is on her flank. Brands are registered. The agent who found her looked it up and notified us."

Kevin smiled, even though Melody couldn't see it as he held his new cell phone.

"We're going to take the trailer and pick her up this weekend."

Then Melody told him she was getting her driver's permit. She said she was through with babysitting and had a job at a feed store in Sierra Vista.

Savannah never mentioned dinosaurs again,

although sometimes Kevin saw her looking toward the mountains along the San Pedro River. The sinew strap of the necklace that Irtyshi had given her had turned to powder, too, just as all the prehistoric organic products had done, but the pink shell remained. Mrs. Sinclair picked it up off the floor and put it on the top shelf of Savannah's bookcase where it gathered dust.

Kevin told Mrs. Bowersock he had given the belt with its silver and turquoise buckle to a new friend because he had outgrown it. As he said this, he hoped he was wearing his poker face. When she asked if his friend would appreciate it, he nodded an emphatic "yes!", which satisfied her. Shortly thereafter, Kevin's parents decided he was responsible enough to look after his sister, and Mrs. Bowersock was only called upon for Savannah when Kevin wasn't home.

The new topic of conversation at school was about a drone someone had crashed into the cafeteria window during lunchbreak. Thus it was that modern technology topped the story of Kevin's visit to the Pleistocene. Sometimes he wondered if he really had been there. One day he opened the drawer of his desk to put something inside it and pulled out the note his mother had written about the strange bird Mr. Mason had found. Thinking this would be proof he had been in the Ice Age, after all, he read it again: "Petrels and seabirds blown off course from storms in the Sea of Cortez are recuperating at wildlife centers across southern Arizona." Nothing about the Miocene or a giant, bony-toothed prehistoric seabird.

And yet, every now and then when he looked out of his bedroom window, he would not have been surprised to see a caveman in the backyard.

FIN

ACKNOWLEDGMENTS

I am truly grateful to the people who made this book possible. A huge thank you to Dusky Loebel, my editor par excellence, who read so many drafts I have lost count. A special acknowledgement to Allen Denoyer, Preservation Archeologist, for advice on our first Native Americans and for teaching me how to make my own obsidian projectile point and atlatl at his workshops at Archaeology Southwest. Thanks also to Allen's son, Nathan, who kid-tested the story and made awesome suggestions. Thank you to Barbara Lehmann and her dog, Mitzi, who provided the inspiration for her namesake in the story, and to Beverly Malnar and Sam Turner, enthusiastic supporters of this project.

To my husband, Richard, thank you for visiting the Murray Springs Clovis Site with me for the first time four years ago and your unwavering enthusiasm for my story.

Written this day, April 29 2021, our 20th wedding anniversary.